Other Books By Priscilla Baker

I0620900

Cover Design by Melody Simmons

*For my Dad, who spent all those years hauling me
back and forth from my riding lessons*

Dead for Success

Priscilla Baker

The Legend of Bellamy Cove

It was a dark and stormy night in April of 1717. Legendary pirate Black Sam Bellamy, so called for his jet-black hair, was aboard his flagship, the Whydah, racing up the Massachusetts coast. He was eager to reach Provincetown, at the tip of Cape Cod, and reunite with his lover, twenty-one-year-old Mary Hallett.

In his haste, Black Sam ignored the storm brewing around him: whipping wind, arching waves, and streaks of lightning flashing across the sea. Without warning, a massive wave crashed over the bow of the ship, driving it underwater and into the sea bed. With a terrible crack, the ship broke apart, coming to rest under the water only a few hundred feet from the outer shore of Cape Cod. Screams and cries for help filled the night air as men were washed overboard, but there was no one near enough to hear.

As his men drowned around him, Black Sam struggled to shore, dragging with him a small stash of silver coins he'd managed to keep hidden from the crew. Arriving on the beach, he collapsed to his knees, coughing up the sea water that had nearly claimed his life. Staggering away from the water, Black Sam dug a shallow hole, burying the small sack holding what remained of his treasure.

Recovering from his near death, Black Sam made his way on foot to Provincetown, where he was reunited with his lover. After taking the name of his wife, Hallett, the couple returned to the wide beach where the Whydah had gone down, searching fruitlessly for Black Sam Bellamy's buried silver. As they searched, the couple built a small farm, which eventually gave rise to a village. Under the guise of honoring the dead pirate Black Sam Bellamy, Sam and Mary Hallett named the town Bellamy Cove. The Hallets lived out their life on their farm, dying peacefully and passing the land to their children. Today, the Hallett family still reigns as one of the founding families in Bellamy Cove.

Chapter 1

_____Penny Bowden stood in the center aisle of her recently-purchased barn, hands on her hips, taking in the state of the building. One of the fluorescent lights overhead flickered, and the paint on nearly every surface was peeling. *I gave up my nice, new, air conditioned condo for this*, she thought to herself, glancing through the open barn door to the equally run-down house across the yard. Behind her, one of the horses let out a soft whinny from its stall.

"What's that, River?" Penny asked, crossing the aisle to stroke the nose of the gray mare, warm against her hand even in the hot, humid air. She had her head hanging out over the stall door, looking for attention - or just a treat.

It was worth it. She ran her hand over the horse's muscular neck.

Penny leaned against the wall, still idly stroking the mare's neck, as she contemplated all the work that needed to be done.

"Redo the tack room, add a wash stall, repaint, new stall doors..." Penny listed off, speaking to herself. River whinnied again, as if in understanding. "Are you ready to go outside, girl?" Penny asked, unlatching the door to the stall and letting herself in.

Each stall had two doors—one to the aisle, and one out to the pasture, which was located next to the barn, stretching the length of the property.

Penny crossed the stall and opened the back door. "Go on, girl!" she urged, swinging it wide open. The horse trotted through to join her stablemate, a bay gelding named Zion. "Named after the national park," the lawyer who handled the sale of the property had explained about the horse's unusual name. Penny followed, stepping out into the warm, sun-lit pasture - a long, narrow field running along her property between the road and the red painted barn. On the other side of the barn sat a riding ring, perfect for giving riding lessons, and behind the barn was a small round pen.

Penny turned away from the horses, noting that the sign on the side of the barn reading *Seashore Stables* was hanging low on one side. "Add that to the list," she muttered to herself, heading back into the stall and latching the stall door behind her. She pushed her long red hair, tied up into a ponytail, back over her shoulder.

Penny had purchased the property, sight unseen, as a "fully operational" lesson stable, located in the small town of Bellamy Cove, Massachusetts. It came fully equipped with a house, barn, pasture, lesson ring, and two horses. It also came with Joe Pipps, a stablehand who lived in a small apartment over the barn. Even though she could only afford to pay him a pittance, he'd agreed to stay on in exchange for the free rent. Penny had arrived earlier in the week and had barely begun to unpack. With her financial know-how, a remnant of her previous career, and her horse knowledge, from growing up on a ranch in Montana, Penny had big plans for the Seashore Stables.

Penny crossed the stall, returning to the large central aisle of the barn. It had a concrete floor and ran from one end of the barn to the other, with a large, sliding door on either side. "Hey, Joe?" she called out, looking for her stablehand.

"Yes, Ms. Bowden?" he answered, coming down the stairs from his tiny apartment. He was an older man, stooped with age, but he still worked harder than anyone Penny had encountered at the financial firm she had just left.

"Joe, please, call me Penny." She smiled. "I'll never remember to answer to Ms. Bowden."

"Sure thing, Penny," he replied, almost reluctantly as he ran a hand through his short gray hair. "What can I do for you?"

"I'm going to run into town and pick up some paint for the interior of the barn. Would you mind getting started with scraping off the old paint?" Penny requested. "It's a good day for it. Nice and warm, so the horses can spend the night in the pasture and we can get the whole barn done today and tomorrow."

"I'll get started right away," Joe promised. "I should be able to get it done today. This paint is so old it'll come off if you breathe on it."

"Thanks, Joe," Penny told him gratefully, heading out to the yard.

Her blue Jeep, which she had purchased used at the same time she bought the farm, was parked next to the small house. Penny still couldn't get used to driving again; back in the city she had just taken the subway everywhere. *Oh well*, she thought to herself, looking at the vehicle with just a flicker of doubt. Climbing into the old Jeep, Penny started it up, letting out a tiny sigh of relief when it roared to life. It hadn't failed on her yet, but its appearance did not inspire confidence.

Driving down the lane that led out to the main road, Penny couldn't help but smile as she caught a glimpse of the shimmering blue sea through the trees. *That, right there, is what makes all this worth it.* She rolled the windows down, taking a deep breath of the hot, salt-tinged air.

Growing up in Montana, Penny had always been fascinated by the ocean. The first time she had seen it, on a family vacation to California, she knew she was destined to be near it. She'd begged her parents to sell the ranch and move to the beach, but alas, no such luck. She'd spent her childhood and teenage years grabbing any chance she could get to be close to the ocean, which usually meant trips to visit a crotchety old aunt who lived on the Oregon coast. When it came time to go to college, Penny had only applied to schools in coastal cities, and had ended up in Boston.

Smiling at the memory, Penny continued driving down the main road, quickly reaching downtown Bellamy Cove—or at least, what the locals thought of as downtown. There were a few small shops, a grocery store, a post office, a bakery, and the town library, along with a few retail stores that only opened in the summer for the tourists. Right now, in late August, the area was always busy, with families flocking to the small beach town for one last hurrah before school started up again.

Carefully navigating her way through downtown, Penny continued a few miles further, to a small combined farm and hardware store on the outskirts of town, a low, long building set back into an otherwise-empty field. The name always made her smile - Jack's Farm Emporium.

Penny parked the Jeep and headed inside. She greeted the owner, Jack Lawrence. He was an older man, with short grey hair and deeply tanned skin. Even though she'd only been in town for a week, she'd already gotten to know him—and his store—quite well. Penny had a feeling she'd be spending a lot of time there.

She headed directly to the small paint section at the back of the store.

"Looking for anything special?" Jack called over from the counter at the front.

"Joe and I are going to repaint the barn," Penny told him. "A fresh coat of paint will really help liven up the place, I think."

"Good for you," he said with an encouraging smile as he approached the paint section. "That farm needs a young person to bring it back to life. Old man Collins tried his hardest to keep it running; but after his wife died a few years back, he just lost his energy," Jack explained, shaking his head. "Joe tried his hardest, but you can't run a place like that all on your own. Especially if you're not the one holding the purse strings."

"I'm going to do my best," Penny promised. "I can tell how beautiful it used to be, back when it was fully operational. I'm hoping to get it there again someday," she told him, turning a can of paint to read the label.

"So what color were you thinking?" Jack asked, getting down to business. "I have plenty of this white, if you're interested." He gestured to the can Penny's hand was still resting on. "I'd estimate you'll need about eight or nine cans for that barn of yours."

Penny couldn't help but smile. *It's going to take some getting used to, remembering what it's like to live in a small town where everyone knows everything. Including the size of my barn,* she mused.

"Is this...uh, your least expensive option?" Penny asked hesitantly. Purchasing the farm and Jeep, along with restocking all the hay and feed for the horses, had nearly wiped out her savings account.

"It is," Jack responded, heading back to the front counter. "I'll even throw in a few cans of green for an accent color, on me. Consider it a housewarming gift."

"Thank you," Penny replied gratefully. "But you'll put the white paint on my account, right?"

"On the account," Jack echoed, nodding as he entered the items into his cash register. "Like I told you last time, I'll just send you the bill at the end of the month. Let me grab my son, Patrick. He'll take these cans out to your car." Not waiting for Penny's response, he turned and shouted over his shoulder, "Patrick!"

A moment later, a man with tousled brown hair emerged from the office behind the counter. "Yeah, Dad?" he asked, coming around the counter.

"Patrick, please help Penny here with these paint cans," Jack requested. "Nine of the white here, and grab her four of the green as well, please."

"You got it, Dad!" Patrick replied with a cheery grin, getting to work.

"I don't know what I'd do without those boys," Jack told Penny. "He and my other son, Sam, they do all the heavy lifting for me these days. One day, they'll own this place," he continued, almost wistful.

"That's lovely. I love to see all the family operations here in Bellamy Cove."

They were interrupted by Patrick returning from the parking lot. "You're all set, ma'am," he told Penny, his brow now damp with sweat. "Have a wonderful day!"

Penny left the cool air-conditioned store and climbed back into the Jeep, heading back to the farm. *Back home*, she corrected herself. She still thought of the condo she had shared with her soon-to-be ex as home, even if she would never see it again. At the very least, he had been forced by the lawyers to buy out her half of it, providing Penny with the financial means to feed the horses through the winter.

Penny had big plans for the stable. She was hoping to offer riding lessons year-round to the local kids, with additional trail rides and lessons for tourists in the summer. *Maybe by next summer, I'll be able to buy a few more horses*, she mused as she headed back towards town.

As she approached downtown Bellamy Cove again, the grocery store came into view. It was a big store, one of the only chain stores located in Bellamy Cove. Penny realized she had nothing in the house for dinner, and quickly flipped on her turn signal and pulled into the parking lot.

Finding a spot, she hurried inside, intending to just pick up a few things. She was immediately greeted by a large folding table in the entryway, festooned in pink streamers. There were three women stationed behind it, chatting as they sipped take-out cups of coffee.

A banner hung across the front of the table. It read, "Bellamy Cove Annual Bake-Off--Support the Fire Department!" A *bake-off*? Penny thought to herself. *That could be fun.* She approached the table, shivering slightly in the mechanically-chilled air.

"Hello, ladies," she said, greeting them hesitantly as they turned to face her. Penny nervously raked a hand through her straight copper-colored hair. "Shiny as a new penny," is how her father had always described it.

"Hello!" cried the woman all the way on the left. "Are you interested in entering the bake-off? We're hoping for a few last minute entrants," she explained with a perky smile, brushing a piece of her shoulder length blonde hair behind her ear. Her face was round, with cupid's-bow lips and a button nose. She looked to be around Penny's age, in her mid-thirties.

"It *is* tomorrow," interjected the one on the right, the oldest of the group. She had a short crop of grey hair, shining against her dark skin, and high, distinguished cheekbones. "Not a lot of time, we know."

"I'd love to. I make a great cherry pie," Penny volunteered, a shy smile on her face.

"And you'll still be here tomorrow, right?" the woman in the middle asked. She had a neat blonde bob haircut, and an angular face, her features sharp. Her voice was loud, almost painfully loud in the tiny store entrance. "We have a lot of people who enter the contest without realizing their vacation ends before it begins."

"I will," Penny declared firmly. "I expect to be here for a long time. I just purchased Seashore Stables," she explained.

"Oh," the woman in the middle exclaimed loudly, laying down her pen. "In that case, I sold it to you!" she explained, a big smile spreading across her face. "Caroline Collins. Seashore Stables was my father's place, until he passed away recently. Nice to meet you in person." She reached out to shake Penny's hand. "And you're...Penelope, correct?"

"Penny, please. Only my mother calls me Penelope," Penny corrected the other woman.

"Penny, then. This is Lucinda," Caroline told Penny, gesturing to the older woman on the right. "And this is Emma," she gestured to the blonde woman on the left. "Do you like to bake?" Caroline asked curiously.

"I do," Penny confirmed, confused by the looks the three women were sharing. "That's why I want to enter the competition," she explained, feeling like she was stating the obvious. "And, of course, to get to know everybody in town," she added quickly. "Maybe make some friends," she continued, her voice trailing off.

"And you plan on sticking around Bellamy Cove?" Lucinda asked cautiously, glancing at the perky blonde named Emma.

"I do," Penny said again, more firmly this time. She may have been confused by their line of questioning, but she didn't want them thinking she wasn't here to stay.

"That's good to hear," Lucinda chimed in with a kind smile, her voice warm. "Welcome to Bellamy Cove. Why don't you set up with us at the bake-off tomorrow?"

Penny returned the older woman's smile. "That would be great, thank you."

"Our pleasure," Caroline replied, waving a hand through the air. "You'll get to meet the fourth member of our group, as well. She owns the local bakery."

"That sounds fun," Penny replied, her smile spreading across her face and lighting up her honey-colored eyes. "I'm looking forward to it."

"I should warn you about the bake-off," Lucinda informed Penny, growing serious. "There's a terrible group of old biddies in town. They all think very highly of themselves, and they *hate* newcomers—especially newcomers who try to butt in on town tradition."

"But don't worry," Caroline reassured her. "We'll be there to protect you from Janine and her cronies."

"Who's Janine?" Penny asked, not sure she wanted to know the answer.

"Janine Hallett," Lucinda explained. "She's descended from the original Hallett family, the ones that founded Bellamy Cove. Janine thinks she's the town queen."

"Janine is also the leader of the Grouchy Old Ladies, as we like to call them," Emma jumped in, her voice sincere and sweet even as she warned Penny. "But don't worry. They're harmless, they just hate change," she advised. "They'll get used to you eventually, once you prove you're sticking around."

"Well, thank you for the warning, but I'm not afraid of a few old ladies," Penny told them, her voice confident. "I'd better get shopping. I guess now I have a lot of baking to do tonight!" she added cheerfully. "Will I see you all at the bakeoff?"

"Of course," Lucinda said. "Good luck!"

Penny moved away from the table, smiling to herself and mentally adding all of the ingredients for cherry pie to her shopping list.

Chapter 2

That evening found Penny hard at work in the farmhouse's small kitchen after having spent the day painting in the barn with Joe. George Collins had left the house, and kitchen, well equipped, but it was sorely lacking in counter space. "One day, I'll have to get around to remodeling in here, too," Penny muttered to herself. The counters themselves were a light-tan laminate, and the cupboards and appliances a deep brown. In fact, the whole house was decorated in different shades of brown.

Penny had just finished her evening meal—a frozen meal heated up in the microwave—and was elbow-deep in pie crust. She was an excellent baker, but a cook she was not.

Methodically rolling out the crust, Penny mentally went over her checklist of work to be done, adding to it as she glanced around the farmhouse. It was small but serviceable, with a kitchen, small dining room, and living room on the first floor, and two small bedrooms on the second. The front door opened out onto a small porch, and a back door opened onto the tiny strip of grass which separated the house from the trees behind it. There was an attic as well, but Penny hadn't yet ventured up the rickety ladder to explore it. *Save that for another time*, she'd decided on the day she moved in. The house needed some work, but it was more than livable, and that was all Penny was after when she bought it. There were still boxes scattered all over the house; Penny may not have brought much furniture, but she'd been astonished at the amount of clothing she'd discovered she'd owned.

Penny carefully unrolled the pie crust into the tin and began to spoon her homemade cherry filling over it. She'd spent nearly as long trying to find the tin in her still-packed boxes as it had taken to make the filling itself. The recipe had started out as her grandmother's, and then it had become her mother's, and finally Penny's, when she had added her own twist. *The secret ingredient*, she thought to herself as she carefully drizzled an ounce of bourbon over the top of the filling.

Finally, she sliced the remaining pie crust—homemade, of course—into strips and carefully wove a lattice to lay over the top of the whole thing. "Perfect," Penny muttered to herself as she crimped the top layer of crust into the bottom around the edge. With a little flourish, she sprinkled coarse brown sugar over the whole thing.

It is strange being the only one in the house. I didn't used to talk to myself so much - Paul was always there to answer, she realized, thinking of her nearly-over marriage. *When times were good, we had a lot of fun.*

Penny's thoughts were interrupted by a loud *bang*, coming from outside the house. She paused, cocking an ear towards the door. When the noise was followed by a loud whinny from the pasture, she stepped away from the kitchen counter, brushing the flour from her hands and hurrying out the front door into the night. She quickly crossed the yard to the pasture gate.

"Well, you two look just fine," she observed, speaking to the horses as she arrived at the field. "What's the matter?" she asked, stroking Zion's deep brown neck. He had come right to the gate to greet her, while River was in the middle of the field. Darkness had settled over the farm completely, but a light shone out of the lower level of the barn. *That's strange.* Brow furrowed, Penny hurried to investigate. Stepping into the barn, she discovered Joe hard at work, still painting.

"Oh, Joe, you don't have to work all night!" Penny exclaimed. "It's late. You're off the clock!"

He gave her a polite smile. "I figured, if I get this coat done tonight, I'll just have to do one more tomorrow morning and the horses can come back inside."

"Makes sense," Penny admitted. "Can I help?"

"No, no," Joe protested, waving the paintbrush. "I just have this wall to finish. I'll be done in a jiff," he promised.

"In that case, I'll get back to my pie," Penny told him, her tone relieved. "Are you planning on coming to the bake-off in town tomorrow?" Joe didn't seem like the civic type, but in small towns like this it was always tough to tell.

"I'm there every year, ma'am," he said with a grin, the first real smile Penny had seen from him. "My dad was part of the fire department, so I do what I can to help them out. Pay ten bucks, and eat as much dessert as you want? It's a dream come true!" he continued with a laugh. "I've been going since I was a boy."

"I'm glad to hear it! I'm entering tomorrow—it'll be my first real outing in Bellamy Cove. I'll save you a slice of cherry pie," Penny offered with a smile. Penny turned to go back in the house, before pausing for a moment as she remembered her reason for coming outside in the first place. "Did you hear a loud noise right before I came out?" she asked curiously. "I heard a loud noise, and then one of the horses."

"That was my fault," Joe admitted sheepishly. "I knocked the ladder over, gave them a spook."

"Oh, good. I was worried it was some part of the barn falling down," she added with a laugh. "Have a good night!" she called out as she left the barn and headed back to the house.

Back inside the cozy farmhouse, Penny gave her hands a quick wash before popping the pie in the oven and settling back into her favorite armchair, one she had stolen from her parents' ranch and had shipped across the country. Paul had always hated it—its thick, cozy cushions and bright geometric pattern interfered with the 'modern' look he was so fond of. He had relegated it to the spare room, but here in the farmhouse it was on display front and center. Penny had positioned it near the big picture window in the living room, so that when she sat down to have her morning coffee she could sit back and watch the horses graze. So far, that morning ritual was one of her favorite parts of her new life.

Penny smiled to herself, leaning back in the chair. For all the changes it had taken to get here, she had never imagined that one day, she'd be living out her childhood dream. Owning her own farm, near the ocean, with a few horses that she knew by name.

As much as she had enjoyed growing up on her parents' ranch, it had been a working cattle ranch, and there had been no room for sentimentality. Penny had fled to the east coast for college as soon as she could, looking for a different way of life and assuming she was done with farms forever.

Life has a funny way of tricking you like that, Penny mused as she closed her eyes. She drifted off to sleep, only being startled awake a short while later by the timer she had set for the pie.

"Oh, shoot, shoot, shoot!" she muttered, hurrying over to the oven. She pulled the door open, only to see that the pie was the perfect shade of golden brown - no panic necessary. *Phew*, Penny thought as she slipped on her oven mitts.

The pie safely settled on the cooling rack, Penny switched off the oven and headed upstairs to her bed. *Have to get a good night's sleep before the bake-off tomorrow!* She thought to herself, smiling in the darkness as she climbed the stairs.

Chapter 3

Waking early the next morning, Penny kept her eyes closed for a moment as she lay in bed, marveling at the peaceful sounds of her new life. She could hear the gentle clinking of metal on metal, the sound of Joe letting the horses out into the pasture, and the chirping of birds in the yard. *So much better than the honking and shouting I used to wake up to in the city.*

Suddenly, Penny remembered what day it was. "The bake-off!" she exclaimed into the empty room. She jumped up, quickly getting ready for the day and hurrying downstairs. She was dressed in her favorite blue sleeveless top, which set off her red hair, and a pair of khaki shorts.

Penny smiled as she reached the bottom of the stairs and saw the pie sitting on her counter, exactly where she'd left it. A shaft of sunlight was beaming in through the large picture window, highlighting the golden pie against the dark counter.

Penny waltzed over and inhaled deeply, filling her lungs with the sweet scent of the pie. "Perfect!" she declared. As she leaned over the counter, Penny was distracted by a movement in the corner. *Oh no. Are there mice in this old house?* She crossed the room to investigate.

A little furry tail was wrapped around the base of Penny's armchair, the rest of the animal hidden behind it. Penny nervously poked her head over the top of it and discovered one of the barn cats, peering up at her.

"What are you doing in here?" she asked in surprise. "You're a barn cat, that means you live in the barn," she told it firmly. Penny crossed the room and opened the front door. "Go on, outside!"

The cat stared back, not moving an inch. "Shoo!" Penny commanded. The orange cat responded by rolling onto its side and stretching out, revealing a white belly and matching white paws.

"I don't have time for this, get out!" Penny tried again. The cat still didn't move, lolling in the sunlight. "Fine!" Penny huffed in frustration. "I'm leaving now, but you better not break anything!" she told the cat.

Back in the kitchen, Penny wrapped a kitchen towel around the pie, taking care not to damage the crust. She headed out the front door, shooting a dirty look at the orange cat still lounging in the sun.

Penny headed to the barn, stopping at the Jeep to carefully settle the pie in the passenger side footwell.

"Joe?" she called out as she entered, blinking at the sudden darkness after being outside. As her vision adjusted, she saw him at the back of the barn, painting the empty stalls. The barn had six stalls, more than they needed right now for the two horses. Penny had big plans to fill them.

She walked the length of the aisle to meet Joe. "I'm heading into town now. You're still coming to the bake-off, right?" she asked. "It'll be nice to see a friendly face."

"I'll be there!" Joe promised, his voice cheerful. "I just want to finish up this last coat of paint. I only have a bit more to go." He gestured at the small amount of wall he had left to cover.

"Thank you," Penny said gratefully. "I don't know what I'd do without you!" she quipped, smiling. "Oh, by the way, one of the barn cats somehow got into the house. The orange one. It wouldn't leave. Would you mind trying to get him out in a little bit?"

"There's an old cat flap in the back door," Joe explained. "I'll get him out before I leave for the bake-off, but I can't promise he won't go back in. I could replace the door, get rid of the cat flap, if you want me to?"

"No, that's okay," Penny replied. "I guess I'll just have to let them come inside, then," she sighed, resigning herself to a house covered in cat hair.

"Not a cat person, then?" Joe asked with a chuckle.

"I don't mind them. I just prefer them when they're in the barn catching mice. Doing their job," she pointed out.

"Well, truth be told, I do let the two of them sleep on my bed upstairs," Joe confessed. "So they certainly have come to expect their creature comforts."

"I knew you were a softy, deep down!" Penny teased. "That's fine. I'll let you be the farm's go-to cat wrangler," she added with a laugh. "By the way, do the two of them have names?" she asked curiously.

"The orange one is Cheddar, and the grey one is Stilton," Joe explained, watching for her reaction. When Penny raised an eyebrow, he laughed. "George was a big cheese guy. He'd invite me inside sometimes and just have ten or twelve cheeses spread out on the counter, and we'd try them all," he reminisced, smiling.

"Really?" Penny laughed. "I never would have guessed, not based on what I've heard about him," she said thoughtfully. "Oh well. Cheddar and Stilton it is!"

"For now, though, I have to get to the bake-off," Penny continued, checking her watch.

"I'll see you there!" she called back as she exited the barn with a wave.

Penny hopped in the Jeep and started it up. She carefully drove into town, keeping an eye on the pie the whole way. Finally arriving, she parked the car in the small municipal lot and gathered up her precious cargo. The bake-off was being held at the town pavilion, which was at the edge of the town, located on the town green overlooking the water.

The town of Bellamy Cove itself was up on a cliff, towering at least fifty feet over the sea; but the beaches, and the cove itself, were accessible from outside of town. One such access road was across the street from Penny's farm, only a short walk—or ride—away. That had been one of the selling points for Penny when she decided to purchase Seashore Stables.

Her hair whipping in the sea breeze, Penny crossed the town green and approached the pavilion. It was clearly old, but had been lovingly maintained, with the exterior painted a bright white and the inside a soft gray. Inside, she could see the women she had met yesterday, along with a few older women. The pavilion practically sparkled in the morning air against the bright green grass. Penny took a deep breath as she went up the steps, enjoying the tinge of salt in the air.

"Good morning, everyone," she greeted the group, feeling hesitant.

Caroline Collins, the one whose father had owned Seashore Stables, turned to greet her. "Welcome, Penny!" she called out, her shoulder length blonde hair sparkling in the sunlight. She crossed the pavilion and took Penny's arm. "Everyone, this is Penny Bowden, the new owner of Seashore Stables!" she announced. Penny blushed as the group turned to face her.

One of the older women crossed the pavilion. She had gray hair, cut neatly into a bob, and was dressed in a perky sundress. "Hello dear," she gushed, laying a hand on Penny's arm. "Penny, is it?" she asked, expertly inserting herself between Penny and Caroline. Penny nodded mutely as the woman led her across the pavilion, away from the others. "I'm Janine Hallett," the woman introduced herself.

This is the woman the baking club warned me about, Penny realized.

"Now, Penny, I have to ask, what are you doing here?" Janine continued, her voice syrupy-sweet. "Everyone knows that the bake-off is a competition for the town founders only. You can stay and participate in the voting, but I'm afraid that pie will have to go," she decreed, pointedly glaring at the dish Penny was still holding.

Penny blushed again, harder this time. "I can't enter the competition?" she asked quietly, hoping no one else in the pavilion could overhear. *Is this real, or is this why they warned me about her?*

"I wouldn't recommend it." Janine sneered, her voice still sickeningly sweet as she patted Penny's hand. "Why don't you head on home, dear." With that, Janine returned to her table in the pavilion, which was already covered in small plates, each holding a square of fudge. Penny was left standing alone.

Overwhelmed by embarrassment, Penny returned to the top of the stairs, intending to go home and dump her pie in the garbage. *Even if she's lying, I don't want to get involved with this*, she thought, glaring at Caroline. who had been joined by Emma and Lucinda, who she'd introduced Penny to yesterday. There was another woman standing with them, this one tall and thin.

"Penny, where are you going?" Lucinda asked in the voice of a worried mother as Penny descended the stairs.

"Home," Penny choked out, hoping no one could see the tears that threatened to spill out of her eyes.

"Penny, wait!" Emma ran down the stairs after her. "Penny, what did Janine say to you? Did she try to tell you that you can't enter?" Emma asked knowingly, reaching out and touching Penny's arm.

Caroline came down the stairs, joining them on the bright green grass. "She's an awful person. That's her little joke. We keep telling her it's awful, but she does it to someone every year. I'm sorry we didn't warn you," Caroline apologized, shaking her head so her short blonde bob swayed back and forth. Her sharp features were downturned in a frown. "I shouldn't have let her grab you like that."

Penny hesitated. "So I *can* enter?" she asked, hope rising up in her chest. At the end of day, it was just a baking competition, but Penny had really been looking forward to making some friends in Bellamy Cove, and this had seemed like just the way to do it.

"Of course you can," Emma reassured her, a kind look on her round face. "The competition is open to anyone who wants to enter," she proclaimed pointedly, raising her voice so those in the pavilion could overhear.

Janine Hallett and her friends carried on with their tasks, not looking up. With that, Emma and Caroline each looped an arm through one of Penny's, who was still holding her pie. They escorted her back up the stairs and into the pavilion.

"Here, join us at our table," Emma offered, gesturing to a long table topped with several different desserts. It had a banner across the front of it, reading *Bellamy Cove Baking Club* in bold letters. As they reached the table, Lucinda took the pie from Penny, carefully setting it down.

"Don't let that old bat give you any trouble," she advised, squeezing Penny's hand. "Now you're really one of us." She laughed. "Janine Hallett's been terrorizing this town since she could talk."

The fourth woman at the table, the tall one, stepped over. "I'm Jessie O'Shea," she introduced herself, shaking Penny's hand. She had short hair that spiked up from her head, dyed bright blue. "Welcome to the bake-off!"

"Jessie owns the bakery in town," Emma said. "She always has the best desserts, even though, *somehow*, she's never won," she continued, glaring daggers across the pavilion at Janine Hallett and her cronies. "The people who come to the competition vote by writing their favorite on a slip of paper at the exit. But somehow, Janine or one of the other founder families, always wins."

"Founder families?" Penny asked, venturing the courage to speak for the first time since returning to the pavilion. "Janine mentioned those, too. What are they?"

"The four original families that founded Bellamy Cove," Lucinda explained, her voice taking on a school-marm lilt. "The Hallett family, who were the first ones to settle in this area, the Beacon family, who came shortly after, the Clarks, who founded a small boat yard, and the Ellwins, who arrived last," she listed off, raising a finger for each family. "The founding families think very highly of themselves. Those ladies think we all owe them a big favor."

"Oh," Penny said simply, struggling to take in all the information they had just thrown at her. "So, basically, Janine Hallett is the queen bee?"

"Yep!" Jessie and Emma chorused together. "That about sums it up. Did you have any idea you were moving to such a dramatic town?" Jessie asked with a grin.

"No way—I thought this was a peaceful little seaside village!" Penny admitted with a smile, her spirits rising. She brushed a lock of hair from her face.

"There's no such thing," Lucinda replied sagely. "Every town has its fair share of drama and gossip. Ours is just a little closer to the surface."

"Come, have a seat," Caroline urged, beckoning Penny behind the table. "You'll need to slice up your pie before we start, and serve it onto these plates." She held up a stack of tiny disposable plates. "Cut into the smallest pieces you can manage. You want as many people as possible to try it; no one will vote for you if they can't try it first." she pointed out.

Penny moved behind the table and sat down in the folding chair Caroline pushed towards her.

She took the small paring knife offered by Emma and got to work.

As she worked, focused on her slices, Penny failed to notice Janine Hallett approaching from across the pavilion.

"Dearie, I hope you didn't take my little prank too seriously. It was only a joke," Janine said, an edge creeping into her sickly-sweet voice. "It's how we welcome all the newcomers!" she continued with a fake little laugh. "How about I try some of your pie?" she offered, helping herself to a slice.

"Well, if that's how you greet people, I think they should take you off the welcoming committee," Penny replied, keeping her voice steady as she looked up at the older woman. "Because you're not very friendly at all," she snapped, returning to her task.

Janine huffed, her face growing red. "Well, I never!" she declared, spinning on her heel and returning to her fudge-laden table, where her companions swarmed to comfort her, murmuring reassurances. *Must be the Grouchy Old Ladies*, Penny realized, staring after her.

"You just dissed Janine Hallett!" Jessie whispered in awe. "That was amazing!"

Penny laughed. "Sorry, I guess that *was* a little mean. I just don't really take to being bullied. Must be my big city ways," she added sarcastically.

The women laughed. "If that's the case, then I think you might just be exactly what we need around here," Caroline commented.

Soon, the bake-off was underway. Tourists and town residents alike crowded the pavilion, each paying their ten dollar entrance fee in support of the fire department. A photographer with dirty blonde hair circled the pavilion, snapping pictures of kids stuffing their faces and adults beaming with joy.

"Will it be this packed the entire time?" Penny whispered to Lucinda, who was standing on her left with an offering of lemon cookies.

"Yep," Lucinda whispered back, scanning over the limited supply of pie Penny had remaining. "Are you almost out?"

"I didn't think I'd need more than one pie," Penny said. "I had no idea it'd be so crowded!"

"It's the tourists," Jessie chimed in from Penny's right. "This is their last big hurrah before the fall. That's why we always hold the baking competition on the last weekend in August." She handed another guest a plate holding her apparently-famous cranberry cake.

"Makes sense," Penny conceded. Across the pavilion, the line for Janine Hallett's table wrapped halfway around the open-air space. "Is her table always so popular?" Penny asked, gesturing at the line. A younger woman, wearing clothing that looked more expensive than Penny's car, was standing with Janine, helping her pass out plates. She had long, dark hair pulled back into a low chignon and elegant features arranged in a polite smile.

"All the townies know they'd better put in an appearance at her table," Jessie whispered. "Otherwise, they're on the naughty list for the next year. And with all the committees and boards Janine sits on, you certainly don't want to risk that," she added with a wink.

"Who's the woman helping her?" Penny asked curiously. Even though the young woman didn't look thrilled to be there, she was making conversation with nearly every guest, and they all seemed to be leaving the table with a smile.

"That's Lisa Hallett. She's Janine's daughter. In training to be the next queen of Bellamy Cove," Lucinda jested, with just a hint of bitterness in her voice.

"She's lived a life of total luxury, thanks to her mom. Could you even imagine having the money to do that?" Caroline asked, shaking her head.

Across the pavilion, Janine excused herself from the table, leaving her daughter in charge. "I need a break!" she declared, her voice floating out over the crowd. She took a seat in one of the folding chairs arranged around the perimeter of the pavilion.

Penny got back to serving, carefully slicing some of the larger pieces of her pie in half so she could stretch it to serve a few more people. The cherry pie was definitely the least popular dessert at the baking club table, but Penny was proud of how much people seemed to be enjoying it. One woman had even asked for the recipe!

Jessie's cranberry cake was clearly the most popular dish at their table, and she was using every opportunity she could to talk up the bakery she owned in town. *Good advertising*, Penny thought to herself. *Maybe next year I could give out pony rides or something*, she thought with a small smile.

Across the pavilion, there was a sudden crash. Penny leapt to her feet, along with the other baking club ladies, only to see Janine Hallett, who had fallen out of her chair and was writhing, awfully, on the ground.

"Oh my goodness!" Lucinda cried out, reaching for Penny's arm.

Lisa, Janine's daughter, was kneeling next to Janine, holding her hand. One of the off-duty firefighters who was attending the event rushed to

Janine's side, while another took off running across the town green. Penny put her hand to her mouth as she gasped.

Lucinda released Penny's arm and hurried across the pavilion, pushing the tourists out of the way. She reached the other side and pulled the folding table away from Janine, effectively blocking her body from the tourists at the same time. "I used to be a nurse, dear," Penny heard her say to Lisa. She knelt next to the firefighter, who was checking Janine's pulse.

"Call an ambulance," the firefighter directed, his voice terse. He shifted a little, placing his hands on Janine's chest. Lucinda leaned back and slid her cell phone out of her pocket, dialing 911. The firefighter bent down low over Janine's body and began to perform CPR.

The entire pavilion watched as the firefighter worked tirelessly over Janine's body. The only sound was Lucinda's voice, speaking quietly into her cell phone. A moment later, the second firefighter, the one who had run from the pavilion, returned, accompanied by another man. Penny could only assume he was a doctor, based on the bag he was carrying and the way he shooed the firefighter aside to take over the CPR.

"An ambulance should be here in about four minutes," Lucinda told him, holding her cell phone away from her mouth.

The doctor nodded, not speaking as he continued CPR. The two firefighters stepped back, blocking the grisly tableau from view. Penny could only watch, horrified at what such a glorious day had turned into.

Chapter 4

A few moments later, the ambulance arrived, it's mournful wail carrying through the warm summer air. It bounced up and over the curb, heading directly to the pavilion. The vehicle parked and it's crew scrambled out, two running to open the back doors and unload the stretcher while the third hurried to Janine's side.

"Collapse and seizures, unknown cause," the town doctor told the paramedic. He stepped back, letting the new team take over. Lucinda stayed by Lisa's side, her arm around the young woman as they watched the paramedic's load Janine into the ambulance. Lucinda hurried over to rejoin the baking club.

"I'm going to go with Lisa to the hospital," she told them, speaking quickly. "Someone needs to go with that poor girl. I'll call with any updates," she added, grabbing her purse and returning to Lisa's side.

The ambulance left, disappearing as quickly as it had arrived. It was quickly replaced by a black-and-white cruiser, carrying two unformed representatives from the Bellamy Cove Police Department.

Penny sank back into her seat, unable to believe her eyes. "Oh my goodness," she breathed. She watched as Janine's friends, the so-called

'Grouchy Old Ladies', swarmed to the doctors side, peppering him with questions.

"I can't believe it," Emma whispered, as if in shock.

"Did she choke?" Caroline wondered.

"It looked like she just collapsed," Jessie offered in a hushed voice.

"She was eating my pie," Penny realized, noticing the bright red filling smeared across the plate that had fallen out of Janine's hand. "Mine was the only cherry pie," she reminded them, speaking slowly.

"Maybe she choked?" Emma suggested, playing with the end of a lock of her beautiful blonde hair.

"Maybe," Penny agreed, still worrying. "I hope not."

"I'm sure it was just her time," Caroline reassured her, reaching over to rub Penny's arm. "After all, she was awfully old. People go when they're ready."

The doctor approached the baking club table. "Hello," he greeted the group before turning to Penny. "I'm Dr. Perry. I've been informed that the cherry pie was your entry into the bake-off. Is that correct, young lady?" he asked, gesturing to the plate still on the floor.

"I did," Penny confirmed, clenching her fist so hard that her fingernails dug into her palm.

"What was in it?" Dr. Perry asked, frowning. "Anything unusual?"

"Not at all, doctor," Penny assured him. "Cherries, sugar, a little bit of lemon juice, vanilla extract," she listed off, thinking back over the recipe. "And my secret ingredient, which is an ounce of bourbon," she added. "But all the alcohol cooks off," she reassured him.

"Uh-huh," the doctor replied, seeming to chew on his words. "Thank you for the information, miss," he replied politely before crossing the pavilion to rejoin the police officers. One of them scooped up the pie from the ground, carefully depositing it into an evidence bag.

Dr. Perry reached out to shake the hand of one of the officers and strode away, returning to what Penny could only assume was his office on the edge of the town green.

Left without a subject for their relentless questions, Janine's friends seemed momentarily lost. One of them tried to speak to the officers, but was summarily ignored. Instead, the old women seemed to zero in on Penny, bustling across the pavilion.

"You!" shouted one of them, jabbing her finger in the air. "You were so cruel to her you gave her a heart attack!"

"Bullied her into a hospital bed!" accused another, her tightly curled hair almost as blue as the sky.

"Verbally assaulted her, more like!" shrieked the third.

Penny was frozen in her seat, staring up at the three elderly women. "I did no such thing," she managed to stutter out.

"Penny did nothing!" Emma, the perky blonde, leapt to Penny's defense. "Janine bullied her, like she does to everyone, and Penny just defended herself!"

Penny rose from her chair. "Emma's right. That lady was a bully. And so are you," she declared, turning away from the old ladies as her cheeks flushed with anger.

The police officers hurried across the pavilion. "What's going on over here?" drawled the bigger man, his voice thick with a New England accent.

"This young lady verbally assaulted poor Janine earlier today. No doubt gave her a heart attack!" cried the old woman who had spoken first.

The officer held up a hand. "You're that new girl, right?" he asked. "Out on the old Collins place? I'm Officer Calhoun."

"My name is Penny Bowden. Don't listen to these ladies," Penny told the officer firmly. "Janine tried to bully me, and I wouldn't take it. Caroline, Emma, and Jessie were all witnesses. Along with Lucinda," she added, gesturing to the women who had gathered around her.

They were interrupted by a sharp *crackle*. Officer Calhoun grabbed the radio from his belt and held it up to his ear, listening closely. "Go ahead," he told whoever was on the other end.

A second later, he returned the radio to it's holster, a grave look on his face. "Janine Hallett died en route to the hospital."

Penny gasped, sinking back into her chair. Next to her, she heard Jessie do the same, and Emma cry out. Caroline seemed frozen, staring straight ahead with a hand to her mouth.

The Grouchy Old Ladies, on the other hand, had no issues showing their grief. They seemed to collapse into one another, wailing without abandon as they wrapped their arms around each other in the center of the pavilion.

After a moment, Officer Calhoun turned to his partner. "Dawes, this is a crime scene. Bag the rest of that cherry pie, and make sure you keep the piece she was eating separate. We'll need statements from everyone."

His partner nodded, not saying a word.

"We'll have to do some tests on that pie of yours," the officer drawled, turning back to Penny. "And we'll need a statement from each of you before you can leave." He pulled out a small notebook. "Ms. Bowden, you're first."

It was almost three hours before Penny and the rest of her new friends were able to leave the pavilion.

"He thinks she choked on my pie," Penny said miserably as the group made their way across the town green. "That, or I managed to give her a heart attack by standing up to her. Either way, he thinks it's my fault. And so do those terrible old women."

"It'll be okay," Emma said reassuringly, reaching out to wrap an arm around Penny.

"I'm sure they'll find that it was something totally unrelated," Caroline chimed in.

"It was just her time," Jessie added, uncharacteristically kind. Penny could already tell that she faced the world with humor and sarcasm instead of smiles and kindness.

"Why don't I drive you home?" Caroline offered. Jessie can follow us and bring me back to my car, right, Jess?" she asked, with a nod to the other woman.

"Of course," Jessie agreed. "Let's go. We'll make you a cup of tea when we get back to your place. I've never actually been inside that old farmhouse," she commented with a little smile.

A short while later, when they arrived back at the farm, Jessie helped Penny out of the car while Caroline went to go find Joe. He was still in the barn; he hadn't even made it into town for the bake-off yet. Penny watched his expression change as Caroline shared the awful news with him while Jessie hurried her into the house.

"Sit down," Jessie urged, gently pushing Penny into her armchair. "Do you have any tea?" she asked, opening the cabinet next to the stove.

"I don't," Penny admitted. "I still haven't really stocked the kitchen,"she sighed.

"Here, let me get you a glass of water then," Jessie said, grabbing a cup from the draining rack and filling it. She carried it into the living room, handing it to Penny before sinking onto the small loveseat. "And who's this fellow?" Jessie asked, leaning down to stroke the orange barn cat that was still in the house. He had meandered over to greet her.

45

"That's one of the barn cats, Cheddar," Penny explained. "He's not supposed to be in here. Apparently, there's a cat door he uses."

"I think he seems awfully comfortable," Jessie quipped, laughing as the cat hopped up on the couch beside her. He settled in, curling up with his head resting on the throw pillow. "Seems right at home!"

Caroline came in through the still-open door, closing it behind her. "Well, this place looks much the same," she commented, looking around. Penny had negotiated to buy the house with most of the furniture still inside, since she had left all of hers at the condo with Paul. "Even Cheddar is still here, hanging out on the sofa," she remarked, crossing the room to scratch the cat's ears. He leaned into her hand, emitting a deep, rumbling purr.

"Yeah, I haven't done much rearranging, except for adding my chair," Penny admitted, patting the arm of the chair she sat in. "I dragged this thing all the way from my parents' ranch. There was no way I was leaving it in the city," she added with a dry laugh.

"Where did you grow up?" Jessie asked curiously.

"My parents own a cattle ranch in Montana. I came east for school, and I stayed," she explained quickly, not wanting to go into the story of her failed marriage.

"That explains why you bought a farm," Caroline realized, her voice triumphant. When Penny glanced at her, she blushed a little and explained, "I've just been wondering why someone from the city would want to come down here and buy my dad's little farm. No one around here wanted it."

"To tell you the truth, I didn't really care what town I ended up in," Penny admitted. "I just wanted out of the city. I was married, but I'm...not, anymore. I hired a realtor and asked them to find me a farm. I just wanted some land, where I could spread out and have some animals. And to be near the ocean," she added quickly.

"Don't have that in Montana," Jessie tried to joke.

"That's the truth." Penny laughed, shaking her head. "I'm just glad to be here, even if it led to everything that happened today. Thank you both for bringing me home."

"Our pleasure," Caroline replied kindly. "Listen, I have a question for you. Jessie, Emma, and Lucinda and I all have this little baking club. We meet once a month, and our next meeting is actually tomorrow. Would you like to come?"

"I'd love to," Penny told her, feeling just a little bit of happiness sneak in through the feeling of dread that had washed over her at the pavilion.

"Good." Jessie said firmly. "We'll explain everything to you tomorrow, but all you need to know for now is that we meet at seven, and that this month we're meeting at Emma's. She's right in town, at 79 Shoreview Lane. You don't need to bring anything, except a bottle of wine if you're so inclined."

"Thank you," Penny told the two women gratefully. "A night of baking will be just what I need to start feeling better."

Chapter 5

Afternoon found Penny aimlessly drifting around the house, straightening and unpacking. Penny paused to pet Cheddar, who was still lounging on the loveseat. A ray of sunlight was beaming in through the window and the cat was lolling on his back, paws splayed out to the side as he enjoyed it.

Penny glanced out the window, admiring River and Zion, grazing in the pasture. "I'll go get to work cleaning out that tack room. That will help to get my mind off of things," she said, feeling a little silly for sharing her plans with the barn cat who'd taken up residence on the couch. Shaking her head, she headed out the front door, ignoring his indignant stare at the interruption. Outside, she found Joe spraying a hose over the pasture. They hadn't had a drop of rain since Penny's arrival on the Cape, making it a necessary chore.

"Good idea, Joe," she called out as she approached. "Hopefully we get some rain soon and you can take this off your list."

"Sure hope so," he remarked dryly, seemingly undisturbed by the news of Janine's awful death.

Penny left him to it and headed into the barn, where the tack room was located. It was a disaster zone; saddles and bridles piled high, with horse blankets shoved into the corner and a box chock-full of dirty brushes. The items that were being used for River and Zion were separated, and kept in good condition, but everything else was a mess.

Penny sighed, surveying the pile. "Well, there's no time like the present," she reasoned with herself, slipping on a pair of work gloves and snapping open the heavy-duty garbage bag she had brought with her from the house.

What happened to poor Janine Hallett? Penny wondered to herself as she got to work.

As she turned the question over in her head, Penny worked her way to the back of the room, with most of the old tack and equipment ending up in the garbage bag.

A few hours later, the tack room was looking much better. Penny's cleaning had revealed that the back wall was actually filled with saddle racks, one for each stall. She was thrilled to find them - they sure would help to keep the tack room organized.

Penny carefully organized River and Zion's tack, previously stored in the barn aisle, onto the saddle racks. "Time to tackle the blankets," Penny muttered to herself. The horse blankets she had found balled up in the corner had been left there while she worked in the rest of the room.

Penny carefully examined the blankets for damage before gathering them up—quite an armload—and struggling with them back inside the house, where the washer and dryer were located by the back door. She shoved the first blanket into the washer, a full load on its own, and started the machine before sinking gratefully into her chair. The orange cat, still lounging, gazed dolefully at her before settling back to his nap.

Resting for a moment, Penny returned to her earlier thoughts. *I wish I knew more about Janine. And, more than anything, I really, really hope that our little spat didn't have anything to do with her death.*

Penny reluctantly rose from her comfortable chair, preparing to head out to the barn. She paused for a second as a new noise caught her attention.

Penny turned back to face the interior of the house, ready to investigate. The sound was familiar, but she couldn't quite place it. Looking around, Penny took a few hesitant steps towards the back of the house, listening as the sound grew louder. Suddenly, she recognized the sound. *Running water?* Penny grimaced. *It's never a good sign to hear running water when you don't expect it.*

Penny hurried to the washing machine and was dismayed to find a quickly-growing puddle underneath it,overflowing from the top of the machine and streaming down the side. "Oh no, no, no!" she muttered to herself. Cheddar was watching with interest from the sofa.

Penny quickly punched the STOP button on the machine, and the methodical *swish-swish* from inside slowed to halt. Penny looked around frantically for something to soak up the water. *Where on earth did I put the towels?* In a panic, she grabbed one of the horse blankets waiting to be washed and used it to soak up the water.

Penny looked down at the puddle in relief—the flood hadn't been as bad as it looked. *But why did it happen in the first place?*

Penny opened the lid of the machine, grateful that it was an old-style top loader and not a modern front-loader like she'd had in the condo. Nothing looked amiss inside the machine; it was filled with soapy water, and the unpleasant aroma of wet horse was gently wafting from the machine. Wrinkling her nose, Penny closed the lid and pulled the washer away from the wall. She could only manage to pull it away a few inches, but it was enough to get at the drain hose.

Grabbing a mixing bowl from the kitchen to catch whatever spilled from the hose, Penny carefully unscrewed the flexible hose. Some water spilled out from the machine, but nothing at all from the hose. Gingerly sticking her finger into the tube, Penny was able to wiggle loose whatever the blockage was. *Leaves?* She thought in surprise, shaking the blockage loose into the mixing bowl. The tube was absolutely packed with leaves.

"How bizarre," Penny told the orange cat, still watching. "How did leaves get up into the hose, and so close to the machine?" The leaves would have had to get into the plumbing and travel up the pipes, to the house.

Penny quickly got everything reattached and moved the washer back into place. Crossing her fingers, she pressed the *Start* button and watched as the machine came back to life.

Heading into the kitchen, she quickly dumped the leaves in the garbage and cleaned the bowl she had used, keeping a close eye on the washing machine. It was performing perfectly, not a stray drop of water to be seen.

"I'll wait a little longer," Penny remarked to Cheddar, sitting next to him on the loveseat. "Make sure it doesn't start leaking again." The cat looked bored now that the excitement was over. He tucked his head under his paw and went back to sleep.

Half an hour later, the cycle was done, and Penny quickly switched it to the dryer before heading back out to the barn. She hosed off the horse brushes and set them out in the warm sunlight to dry.

Joe entered the barn, whistling appreciatively at the tack room. "Looks great,

Penny," he proclaimed, a smile on his face. "I've never seen it so clean."

"I'd like to get a fresh coat of paint in here to match the one you just finished in the aisle, and one day, I'd like to get some nice engraved nameplates for the saddle racks," Penny told him, thinking out loud. "But it does look a lot better, doesn't it?"

"It really does," Joe told her.

"Not to change the subject," Penny began, "but the weirdest thing just happened with the washing machine, inside the house. The drain pipe was absolutely stuffed with leaves. Do you know if Mr. Collins ever had any issues with the plumbing?"

Joe looked surprised. "Yes, he did, actually," he told her, recovering quickly. "He always talked about how he'd have to rip all the plumbing out one day," he recounted, shaking his head.

"Really? The house inspector didn't say anything about it."

Joe shrugged. "I never took a look at it myself. But I can always help if anything acts up again—just let me know," he offered, smiling.

"Thanks," Penny sighed gratefully. "How long did you work for Mr. Collins?" she asked. It had never crossed her mind to wonder.

"Only a few years. He and I knew each other when we were kids, though, growing up in town. His parents owned this place back then. They used to breed jumping horses," he told Penny. "And then they passed away, and George Collins took it over and turned it into a lesson stable. He only gave a few lessons the whole time I worked here, though."

"Was there a reason?" Penny wondered.

"He was just getting old. He had to hire me because he couldn't handle things anymore, even once he sold the rest of the horses. Even with just Zion and River, he needed the help," Joe revealed. "For a while, I thought I might end up buying the place after he died."

"Well, I'm glad you've agreed to stay on now that I'm here," Penny remarked gratefully, feeling a little awkward. "I'd be lost without you!"

"It's my pleasure, ma'am," he replied quietly, heading towards the stairs to his apartment. He was awfully spry for a man that must be in his mid-sixties, if not older.

Penny turned around, admiring the work she and Joe had accomplished over the last few days. With a new coat of paint, and a tack room that wasn't a maze, the barn was looking better already. The aisle was swept clean, and the piney scent of the clean wood shavings that covered the stall floors filled the air. Penny smiled with satisfaction, managing to forget for just a second what an awful day she'd had.

Her self-satisfied reverie was interrupted by the sound of a car approaching the barn. Stepping out into the yard, Penny watched as a black-and-white cruiser made its way down her driveway. *Oh, great.*

The car pulled to a stop and Officer Calhoun emerged from the driver's seat. He was a big man; Penny couldn't help but think of clowns and clown cars as she watched him extract himself from the car.

"Ms. Bowden," he called out as a greeting, noticing her by the barn door.

"Officer Calhoun, how can I help you?" Penny asked him, trying to be polite. She crossed the yard to meet him next to the cruiser. He was alone this time, unaccompanied by the silent Officer Dawes.

"Ms. Bowden, I've come to inform you that a preliminary examination by the county coroner showed that Janine Hallett died by way of cyanide ingestion," he said, carefully watching Penny's reaction.

Penny held back a gasp. "Cyanide? Are you telling me she was murdered?"

"Yes, ma'am," the officer told her with a sharp nod. "Do you have any insecticide or vermin poison on the premises?" he asked her, pulling a small notebook from his pocket.

"I...I don't know. I only bought the place a week ago. I haven't looked in every nook and cranny," she admitted, nervousness raising the pitch of her voice. "But regardless, I certainly didn't want Janine Hallett dead!" she insisted to the officer, her voice filled with confidence. That, at least, she could say with certainty.

"Have you ever had any dealings with the Hallett family before this morning?" Officer Calhoun asked, ignoring Penny's protests.

"No! I met the woman for the first time at the bake-off. Do you think that I just carry cyanide around with me, in case I run into someone I don't like?" she demanded, almost laughing at the absurdity.

"I don't know, do you?" the officer asked, staring down his nose at her.

"Of course not!" Penny insisted, feeling ridiculous that she was having this conversation at all.

"Can you expand on the verbal disagreement you had with Ms. Hallet before the bake-off?"

Penny blushed. "Well, she played a...prank on me," she began. "They told me she does it to all the new people. She told me I wasn't allowed to enter the bake-off."

"Some of the witnesses stated that you verbally attacked her after she attempted to explain the rules to you," the officer countered.

"Who told you that?" Penny asked, growing indignant. "If it was those old ladies, don't listen to a word they say! Janine was a bully, plain and simple."

The officer raised an eyebrow. "Young lady, I don't know if I'd be talking like that if I were in your shoes," he warned.

"Janine tried to kick me out of the contest, but the ladies from the baking club told me I could stay. Janine apologized to me, saying that she was only teasing," Penny explained, frustrated. "That's how she ended up with a piece of my pie."

"Well, I'm here to inform you not to leave town," Officer Calhoun told her, closing his notebook. "We may be in contact to bring you in for questioning." Without saying another word, he shoved himself back into the cruiser and left the farm, leaving Penny staring after him, mouth hanging open.

Am I actually a suspect in that woman's murder? Penny's thoughts raced, filled with worry, almost panic. *I barely spoke ten words to her! What on earth are they thinking? There has to be someone in town who actually wanted her dead!* Her thoughts were interrupted by Zion's loud whinny, coming from the pasture. Both horses were standing by the barn, eager for their dinner.

"Alright, alright," Penny called to them, thankful for the distraction. At least taking care of the horses would get her mind off of the dread - and fear - washing over her.

Chapter 6

_____The next evening, Penny was eagerly preparing for her first ever baking club meeting. She'd spent the morning mulling over Officer Calhoun's visit, waiting for the phone call he'd promised that would bring her in for questioning. It had never come, and Penny was happy to have something to distract her for the evening.

Per Caroline and Jessie's instructions, she was planning on arriving with a bottle of wine. Except, of course, that she didn't have any in the house. *I'll guess I'll have to make a pit stop at that wine store in town. Better leave a few minutes early.*

Penny climbed into her blue Jeep, eager to see more of Bellamy Cove on her way to Emma's house. She had been downtown enough times, but had never explored the residential neighborhood adjacent to the shopping district. She started the car up and headed down the drive, noticing as she reached the main road that the sign marking her farm was looking a little ragged. "I'll repaint that, too," Penny promised herself before turning up the radio.

She rolled down the windows, enjoying the breeze on the short drive into town as she tried to shake the feeling of dread that had been plaguing her all day. Penny pulled into the parking lot for the wine store, which was located right next to the grocery store, and shut off the car, not bothering to roll up her windows. She hurried inside and was greeted by the clerk standing behind the counter with a cold stare.

"You're the new one, right?" he asked curtly. The clerk was an older man, starting to go gray, dressed in a neat polo shirt and khaki shorts.

"The new one?" Penny repeated, taken aback by his rudeness. "I just moved to town, if that's what you mean. I bought Seashore Stables," she explained, hoping to smooth over whatever perceived slight the man was upset about.

"Yep. So you're the one who killed Janine Hallett?" The clerk crossed his arms.

"Who killed Janine Hallett? Of course not! Who told you that? I only met the woman yesterday!" Penny exclaimed indignantly. *Are those old ladies telling everyone I murdered their friend?*

"I heard that your pie was the last thing she ate before she died, right there on the floor," the clerk said, gesturing through the window of the store at the pavilion on the town green. "Poor woman. What did she ever do to you?" he asked, shaking his head.

"She was a horrible woman," Penny declared, spinning on her heel to face the door. "But I certainly didn't kill her!" She stormed back out into the warm evening air. "The nerve!" Penny muttered to herself as she climbed back into the car empty handed. She quickly navigated to Emma's house and parked on the street out front. She sat in the car for a moment, breathing deeply to dispel her anger, before climbing out.

As she approached the front door, Penny could hear voices and laughter inside. *I must have the right house,* she thought to herself as she knocked on the sage green door. Emma's house was beautiful, a pale yellow saltbox set back from the street, with a garden out front.

A second later, Emma opened the door, beaming. "Come in, come in!" she greeted Penny, stepping back to make room.

Behind her, Penny could see Lucinda and Caroline, already sitting at the island in Emma's seemingly brand new kitchen at the back of the house. In fact, the whole house seemed newly remodeled, with beautiful hardwood floors and furniture that looked pristine. The living room, to her left, was occupied by two small children, a boy and a girl, coloring on a large pad of paper. The interior of the house was just as lovely as the exterior.

"Hi everybody," Penny greeted them, stepping inside. "You'll never believe what just happened to me!" she declared as she slipped off her shoes in the entryway.

"You told Sebastian Harrow that Janine deserved to die!" Jessie declared, arriving behind

Penny and carrying a bottle of wine. She was wearing short sleeves today, revealing a tattoo of a tiny cupcake just below her elbow.

"What?" chorused the women around the kitchen island, Caroline's voice outshining the rest.

"Sebastian Harrow? Was that who that terrible man was?" Penny asked indignantly. "And I did no such thing. I walked in and he just accused me of killing her!" Penny declared as she joined the rest of the group in the kitchen. "And how do you know about it, anyway?" she asked Jessie.

Jessie smirked before answering. "I was right behind you. I pulled into the parking lot as you left; I waved, but I guess you didn't see me. I went inside and Sebastian was only too happy to fill me in on Bellamy Cove's murderous new citizen," she explained, her smirk turning into a grin. "Gossip spreads quickly in this town."

"Murderous new citizen?" Penny exclaimed in horrified shock. "Oh no," she gulped, her shoulders slumping. "Maybe I should just go back to the city. Or back to Montana. Maybe it was a mistake to come here at all," she sighed, giving into her own self-pity for just a second. Emma reached out a sympathetic hand, touching Penny's arm.

"Or maybe I should do something about this," Penny realized, still slouching in her seat. "Maybe I should prove to those stupid cops that I'm not a murderer," she continued, her voice filling with resolve. "Prove that I'm here to stay," she added, sitting up straighter.

"Good for you!" Lucinda chimed in, her voice filled with warm approval. "You're here now, and you'll stay here. People in this town love to gossip. As soon as the police arrest the real killer, people will forget all about it."

"And how long will that take?" Penny asked sarcastically.

"I'm sure they'll figure it out soon enough," Caroline said, her hands flying up into the air. "They have to know that you don't really have a motive. I heard she was poisoned, so that means that someone just slipped the poison into whatever Janine was eating. Which happened to be your pie," she pointed out. "In the meantime, though, we're all here, so let's get baking! Emma, what are we making?"

"Coconut cookies!" Emma declared excitedly, passing out copies of a recipe. "The way it works, Penny, is that we all get a copy of the recipe, and we all make our own batch. At the end, whoever is hosting—and picked the recipe—will pick a winner, and then the winner gets to host next time, and pick the next recipe. Does that make sense?"

"Yeah, I think so. So you won last time?" she asked Emma as she skimmed the recipe. "What did you make?"

"We made German chocolate cake last month, and Emma blew us all away," Jessie informed Penny. "You promised to write down what you did differently for that cake. I'm still waiting!" she prodded her friend.

"I'll write it down for you tonight. But now, let's get started!" Emma declared, opening her pantry. "Help yourself," she told Penny. "We all have the same recipe, but you can make changes or additions, as long as you 'remain true to the spirit of the dish.' And whether or not you've done that is often hotly contested!" She laughed.

"So, Penny, how are you liking Bellamy Cove?" Caroline asked as they got to work, each claiming a spot around the kitchen.

"Well, apart from being accused of murder, I love it so far!" Penny replied, her despondency from a few moments ago forgotten. "The farm is keeping me busy, but I can't wait to start being able to offer riding lessons. I just want to get the place looking a little more neat and tidy before I do."

"I'd like to see it, once it's all fixed up," Caroline admitted, her voice uncharacteristically soft. "It used to be beautiful, when I was a kid, but after my mom died my dad just didn't have the energy anymore."

"You know, I took riding lessons there when I was little," Emma told them as she measured out flour. "It didn't last for very long, because we moved away, but I loved it," she recounted longingly. "I wish I had gone back to it when we moved back."

"Well, you're always welcome to sign up for lessons!" Penny offered with a smile. "I'll even give you a baking club discount!"

"I might be a little past my prime," Emma admitted with a laugh, "but I'll definitely sign the kids up as soon as you're open!" She gestured to her son and daughter in the living room. "They need something to do after school, and I need something to get them out of my hair!"

"I'll be happy to - I've got two horses, so they can even have their lessons together," Penny offered. "But enough of me trying to drum up business!" She waved her hand. "Tell me more about Bellamy Cove," she requested.

"Well, it depends what you want to know!" Lucinda declared. "We told you about the founding families yesterday, and that the Halletts rule the roost around here. There is that old legend about them," she ruminated, raising an eyebrow as she exchanged glances with the other women.

"Oh, don't go telling her that stupid old legend!" Jessie scoffed. "You already told her how the town was founded. Just leave it at that," she said, beginning to scoop cookies out of the bowl of dough in front of her.

"A legend? Tell me! I want to know everything about Bellamy Cove. The sooner I can act like an insider, the sooner they'll stop accusing me of murder. Hopefully," Penny added wryly.

"Well, the legend says that the Hallett family are not, at all, the Halletts," Lucinda began in a mysterious voice.

"Wait, what?" Penny interjected, her hands coming to rest on the counter in front of her as she listened.

Lucinda held up a quieting hand. "The Hallett family is actually the Bellamy family. There was a pirate, Black Sam Bellamy, named for his jet-black hair. He was famous in these parts back in the early seventeen hundreds. He was shipwrecked, right off the coast here, and managed to swim to shore while every other member of his crew drowned."

"And he traveled to Provincetown, a big whaling town back in those days," Emma continued, picking up the story in her sweet voice, "to reunite with his lover, Mary Hallett. They traveled back here, supposedly because Black Sam had buried his treasure on the beach. They took her name, Hallett, as Black Sam was wanted by the British Royal Navy. They built a home and a farm while they searched for his treasure, but never found it," Emma finished dramatically.

"And after a few years had gone by, and the other founding families came to the area," Caroline jumped in, "a small town started to form. And the Hallett family, now well-settled with lots of kids and a successful farm, suggested naming the town Bellamy Cove, after the pirate who had died right off the coast. The other founders agreed, and Bellamy Cove was born."

"Why did they want to name a town after a pirate?" Penny asked, wrinkling her brow. "Didn't they terrorize the coast back in those days?"

"Not Black Sam Bellamy," Lucinda said. "He was very well respected around here. He was smart, and treated his captives well, often releasing them with a silver coin or two for their trouble. If he came across a woman or child on a boat he took, they were brought to a town and let go. Compared to any other pirate, he was a good guy. People liked him, which is why the other founders accepted the idea."

"Okay...so the legend is that the Halletts are really the Bellamys? And so then Janine Hallett was descended from a famous pirate?" Penny asked skeptically.

"That's what the legend says," Lucinda repeated with a shrug as she began to lay her cookies out on the sheet pan in front of her.

"That is quite the legend," Penny mused as she got back to work, finally mixing her dough. "Are any of the other founder families descended from pirates?"

"Nope, they're all just people who came here for one reason or another," Jessie jumped in. "The Gosten's were close to a founding family, right, Lucinda?" she asked the older woman.

"Close to, but not quite," Lucinda told them. "My ancestors arrived about ten years after everyone else, when the town was just a general store and a post office. Janine always made it *very* clear to me that we do not count as a founding family," she laughed.

"So was that why she never liked you?" Emma chimed in, confusion on her round face. "I never really knew why she was so particularly dreadful to you."

"Nope, her real issue with me was that I won the 1972 Bellamy Cove Spelling Bee, and she came in second," Lucinda confessed to the group, leaning forward with a proud grin.

"What?" Emma asked as surprise registered on her face. "That's what all this was always about? A spelling bee?"

"Yep." Lucinda nodded. "A spelling bee when we were twelve years old. The winning word was 'phalanges,' and she got it wrong. She got the 'ph' right, but swapped the first 'a' for an 'e'," she told them, laughing at the memory. "I spelled it correctly and she was convinced I'd cheated."

"Well, did you?" Jessie asked teasingly. "I'd love to know that deep down, you're as bad as the rest of us!"

"I did not!" Lucinda insisted, her false anger betrayed by the smile on her face. "Remember, I knew I wanted to be a nurse. That was around the time I started reading up on nursing, including studying human anatomy. Phalanges are the fingers," she explained to the women, wiggling hers in demonstration.

"So all this time, Janine hated you because you knew what phalanges were back in 1972?" Penny asked, digging her hands into the dough.

"It was stupidly trivial." Lucinda shook her head. "But Janine was the type of person who let it eat her up inside for fifty years," she added, her face serious again.

"She wasn't a good person," Jessie stated, her voice firm. "Time for the oven!" she exclaimed, lifting her tray of cookies as she changed the subject.

"Oh no, I haven't even started scooping my dough yet!" Penny fretted, gesturing at the bowl in front of her. "I'm going to have to practice to get as fast as you guys." She chuckled.

71

"Nonsense!" Emma exclaimed. "It's not a competition. Jessie is so crazy fast because she spends all day working in her bakery. And besides, the oven can only fit one batch at a time, so it's better if we work at our own speeds anyway," she reasoned. "Lucinda, you're next, then me!" she declared, laying out the final cookie on her own baking tray. "Let's throw these in the fridge while we wait so the dough doesn't get too soft."

Lucinda, Jessie, and Emma all departed for the living room, their cookies safely baking away or stowed in the refrigerator, leaving just Penny and Caroline in the kitchen.

"I'm glad to have another slow-poke around!" Caroline laughed.

"This is a lot of fun," Penny remarked as she added the shredded coconut to her cookie dough. "Thank you for inviting me."

"My pleasure," Caroline said graciously. "I was happy to. We're always looking for new blood!"

"I have a question for you," Penny began cautiously. "About the plumbing in the house...do you know if your dad ever had any issues with it?"

"He did, as a matter of fact, lots of issues. So he had it all ripped out and replaced last year. The plumbing you have now is brand new," Caroline explained. "Why do you ask?"

"I just had an issue with it, earlier today," Penny told her, waving a hand. "Somehow, a huge chunk of leaves ended up in the drain tube for the washing machine."

"In the tube?" Caroline raised an eyebrow. "How bizarre. But no, Dad never mentioned anything like that," she added, shaking her head. "Do you have any idea how it happened?"

"I've been thinking about it all day, and all I can come up with is that someone must have shoved them in there. But why?" Penny wondered.

"You think someone put leaves in your drain hose?" Caroline asked, surprised. "Who?"

"Well, that's my question, too," Penny remarked dryly. "It happened before the bake-off, so it's not like one of Janine's friends did it to...sabotage me, or something." Taking a deep breath, Penny changed the subject. "Anyway, I'm sure it's nothing. So did you all grow up here?"

"We did, for the most part," Caroline answered. "We were all born here. Lucinda, obviously, is older than the rest of us. She and I have spent our entire lives here, except for when I was away at law school." Penny smiled to herself as Caroline continued speaking. A *lawyer? That explains why she talks with her hands - and the loud voice, too!*

Caroline continued. "Emma, who is two years younger than me and Jessie, her family moved away when she was in elementary school, and came back in time for her to graduate from high school here. Jessie was born here, but lived in New York City for a while. When she got pregnant, she came back here—it caused quite a stir. But she bought the bakery, and now that her son is done with high school, he works there full time. He hates it, but he needs a job," she added with a grin.

"So you're a lawyer, Jessie owns the bakery, Lucinda is a retired nurse...what does Emma do?" Penny asked as she began to scoop out her cookies and drop them on the sheet pan in front of her.

"Emma stays home with the little ones, for now," Caroline answered. "She was working at the bakery for Jessie, but she stopped when the kids were born. Emma's bored, though," Caroline revealed, gazing into the living room where Emma was sitting with the kids, helping them color.

"She loves those two more than anything, but her husband is barely here since he commutes into Boston, and she just needs something to do. Otherwise, she's going to mother those two into hating her!" Caroline added with a laugh.

"Maybe business at the bakery will pick up, and she can go back to that," Penny mused. "Or I'm sure there's always seasonal work, right? Things must be way busier now than they are in the winter."

"That's for sure. Have you ever been to a tourist town in the off season?" Caroline asked as she switched the trays in the oven, taking out Jessie's batch and putting in Lucinda's. Penny moved the cooling rack that Emma had left out, allowing Caroline to set down the cookies without having to turn around.

"I haven't," Penny admitted.

"It's very different," Caroline warned her, pouring them both a glass of wine. "Most things are shut down, and a lot of people leave town. There are a lot of people who can't handle the winter out here."

"I grew up on the Montana plains," Penny reminded them. "Trust me, I can handle winter!" she added with a laugh.

"Alright, alright, I believe you!" Caroline laughed as Penny stowed her unbaked cookies carefully in the fridge with the other batches. "Now let's go join the others for a well-deserved break before we sample our masterpieces."

✳ ✳ ✳

Chapter 7

Nearly two hours later, the women had returned to the kitchen island to eagerly taste the cookies, with Emma serving as judge.

"So Penny, tell us about you," Emma requested. "You've heard all of Bellamy Cove's dark secrets," she pointed out with a laugh. "What made you want to move to this little town?"

"Well, like I was telling Jessie and Caroline yesterday," Penny started, taking a sip of her wine, "I didn't even know Bellamy Cove existed until a few weeks ago. I hired a realtor and just asked them to find me a farm somewhere near the ocean."

"But why did you want to leave the city at all?" Jessie prodded, picking up another cookie.

"I'm in the middle of getting divorced," she admitted to the group, blushing a little as she admitted that she'd been unable to keep her marriage together.

"Oh honey, I'm sorry to hear that," Lucinda said gently, reaching out to stroke Penny's hand. "What happened?"

"We just...drifted apart," Penny sighed, not wanting to air her dirty laundry in front of her new friends. "We were both working too much, we didn't have any of the same interests, and we would go days without saying a word to each other. It just wasn't right."

"So you left the city altogether? What about your job? It sounds like it was stressful," Caroline jumped in.

"Yep. I decided I would start over. I was a stock broker at one of the big financial firms, but I quit and spent just about every dollar I had to buy Seashore Stables," Penny told them. "Maybe not my best decision, financially speaking," she admitted, looking down at the beautiful quartz countertop, "but, hey, everybody deserves a midlife crisis, right?" At that, the group all broke into smiles.

"We sure do," Caroline said, shaking her head.

"And anyway, here I am! Enough about me. Who's the winner, Emma?" Penny asked, changing the subject.

"I declare..." Emma began, drawing the moment out. "Lucinda as this month's winner!" The group of women burst into cheers for their friend. Penny joined in, happy to feel included.

"Congratulations!" she cried out. "So this means that next month, we'll meet at your house?" she asked Lucinda.

"Correct. I live way outside of town, in an old house. Out past Jack's store," Lucinda explained, using a landmark that Penny might recognize. "I'll give you directions when the time comes," she added, patting Penny's hand again. "And I don't want to hear any more out of you about a midlife crisis! You're not even close to old enough to have one of those." She laughed.

"So, Penny, are you feeling better now after your encounter with Sebastian?" Jessie cut in.

"I am." Penny smiled. "You guys are pretty good at cheering a person up."

"We try!" Emma exclaimed around a mouthful of cookie.

"I still can't figure out why the police think I did it," Penny continued. "I only met Janine yesterday! There must be someone in town who had a better motive," she added, shaking her head.

"Well, there's always the fact that she was about to sell the landing site," Lucinda volunteered. "The historical society was awfully worked up about that."

"What's the landing site?" Penny asked, picking up another cookie.

"It's the stretch of beach where the legend says that Black Sam Bellamy came ashore and buried his treasure. It's been in the Hallett family ever since then, as part of the estate, but Janine was going to sell it to a developer. It would have been vacation homes by next summer," Lucinda replied. "Or still will be, if Lisa goes through with the sale. She's the oldest child, so everything will go to her." She turned to Penny, explaining, "Janine's husband, David, died years ago. The first born always inherits in that family."

"But if that land is so important, why is she going to sell that particular piece of property?" Penny asked, wrinkling her brow.

"Since it's waterfront, it's definitely the most valuable part of the estate," Caroline volunteered, cookie crumbs sprinkling down as she waved her hands. "But I don't know why she needed the money."

"The historical society had plans to build a monument to Black Sam there," Emma added. "But if it's sold, then obviously not. Plus, no one has ever found the treasure!" she continued with a grin. "If they build houses over it, no one ever will."

"Well, maybe they have the wrong piece of beach," Penny mused.

"Maybe. But it's the only piece of beach connected to the Hallett estate, and why would Sam and Mary Hallett have bought if it wasn't so they could recover his treasure?" Emma asked before stuffing another piece of cookie into her mouth.

"Maybe they just liked the beach!" Caroline exclaimed from across the kitchen island, waving her hands in the air to emphasize her point. "Or maybe Black Sam continued his pirating ways and needed access to the water. But could you imagine finding that treasure?" she asked the group, a note of longing in her voice. "You'd never have to work again; we could retire to some tropical island!" She sighed.

"What is the treasure supposed to be, anyway?" Penny wondered. "Does anyone have any idea what it is? I doubt Black Sam Bellamy could have lugged a treasure chest off of a sinking ship and taken it to shore."

"No one knows," Lucinda said. "That's part of the mystery. Even if something is buried, it could just be a statuette, or a jewel, or silver," she explained. "Bellamy spent a lot of time in the Caribbean, where the Spanish had huge silver mines. That's what a lot of the pirates were after in those days - Spanish silver."

"How do you know all this?" Penny asked, wrinkling her brow. "Are you a big pirate fan, or something?" She laughed.

The women all laughed as well. "No, no," Lucinda corrected Penny, shaking her head. "I was a teacher for a few years while I saved for nursing school. Around here, we teach a lot about pirates and Black Sam Bellamy," she added, grinning knowingly at the younger women who had grown up in Bellamy Cove. *Ah, well that explains Lucinda's well-honed motherly instinct,* Penny realized.

"I loved that part of history class!" Emma beamed, her blue eyes sparkling. "I always thought it was so interesting that pirates had sailed in our waters, way back when."

"And I hated it," Jessie jumped in with a smile. "Well, actually, I guess I hated most of the classes." She shrugged, still smiling.

"You certainly weren't the best student," Lucinda teased, her voice warm.

"Anyway, you should go over and check out the landing site, where Black Sam Bellamy first came ashore and supposedly buried his treasure," Emma suggested to Penny. "It's not far from your place at all. The Hallett family lets the public onto that part of their land, since the beach itself is public."

"Maybe I'll ride over there tomorrow," Penny decided. An idea popped into her mind. "Emma, would you like to come with me? I'd be happy to give you a refresher course on riding," she invited. "My two horses are both super gentle, and we could spend some time in the ring before we head over to the beach if you want. I'll need a guide to make sure I don't get lost in the wilds of Cape Cod." She smirked.

"I'd love to!" Emma exclaimed, an eager smile on her round face. "But I'll definitely need to be reminded of the basics. I haven't ridden since I was in elementary school."

"Of course," Penny reassured her. "And it'll be nice for me to get back to teaching lessons—I haven't done it since I lived in Montana. I'll introduce you to the horses and you can pick which one you'd like to ride," she offered.

"This'll be so much fun!" Emma declared. "And maybe my husband can take the kids to the beach or something while I'm out," she added, more to herself.

"Where is that husband of yours, anyway?" Lucinda glanced around.

"Oh, he's at the bar," Emma scoffed, waving her hand. "He knows better than to be home on baking club nights. We'd just tease him the whole time anyway!" She grinned.

"Smart man, that husband of yours," Jessie chimed in, smirking. "Speaking of husbands, how are things with that new guy you've been seeing, Caroline?"

"What's this? You're dating someone? Spill!" Emma commanded, topping off her wine glass.

Penny smiled; she had been missing this kind of night with her friends from the city. But this was different - her friends in the city had been sharp, and competitive, always looking to one-up each other. This group of women seemed kind, and warm. *Emma is a total sweetheart, and Caroline seems like a good person to have in your corner. Lucinda is obviously the mother figure. Jessie is the tricky one - she's the most like me, I think. A city girl, here in Bellamy Cove.*

"Oh, it's nothing serious," Caroline protested, waving her hand. "He's an exterminator from Wellfleet. We only met because I was his wife's attorney in their divorce!" She chortled. "But he asked me out, and I thought it could be something fun."

"It sounds like an awful lot of fun!" Emma laughed. "Now, Penny, you must think we're terrible, gossiping like this," she commented, turning to Penny.

"Not at all," Penny reassured her, reaching for another cookie. "I was just thinking how much I've been missing nights like these. The last few months I lived in the city, things were so stressful at home I just didn't have any interest in socializing. I'm really glad you invited me to join," she told the group. "This is a lot of fun."

✳ ✳ ✳

Chapter 8

The next morning found Penny out in the barn, grooming River and Zion before Emma's arrival. Each horse was standing in cross ties, with a rope hooked to either side of their halter to keep them in the center of the aisle. The horses were facing each other, their noses about four feet apart.

"Are you two ready for our first trail ride?" Penny crooned to them as she brushed River. "We're going to go down to the beach, and see how you two like the ocean. If you behave, maybe we'll do some trail rides down there once I get some clients," she continued, idly chattering to the horses.

Penny was interrupted by the sound of a car parking in the yard, followed by footsteps approaching the barn. "Oh, they're beautiful!" Emma gasped as she entered and caught site of the horses.

"Careful," Penny warned as Emma approached Zion's backside. "Stick your hand out and touch the top of his rear as you walk by," she instructed. "That will let him know where you are, since he can't see you back there."

Emma did as Penny had instructed, tracing her hand up Zion's side as she moved along it. "What a sweet boy," she gushed to the horse, stroking his deep brown neck and running her fingers through his black mane.

"That's Zion," Penny told her, "and this is River. They're both super sweet, but you still have to be careful when a horse can't see what you're doing," she added, finishing her task and stroking River's side.

"I'll remember that," Emma promised, still stroking Zion's neck. "Can I ride this guy?" she asked hopefully.

"Of course," Penny answered with a grin. "That's actually perfect, since I haven't gotten to ride River yet. Have you ever tacked up a horse?"

"Yes, but again, it was a long time ago. If you talk me through it I'm sure I can do it, though. Are my clothes alright?" she asked suddenly, looking down at her outfit. "I used to have the fancy riding pants and boots, but obviously that was years ago. I looked online and I read that jeans and sneakers are fine?" she asked, gesturing to her clothes.

"That's totally fine. I always ride in jeans. I'll give you a helmet to wear, though," she told Emma firmly.

"Of course. Maybe one day I'll get myself some fancy cowboy boots like those!" Emma laughed, gesturing to Penny's elaborately embroidered boots. She had dragged them with her from Montana when she moved east, feeling silly, but they were sure coming handy since Penny had moved to the farm.

"You'll need them if you keep coming back!" Penny added, joining in her new friend's laughter. "Now come with me," she directed, waving Emma over. "I'll show you the tack room and what you need to grab for Zion."

"We can just leave the horses like this?" Emma asked, ducking under the cross ties and joining Penny at the door to the tack room.

"These two, absolutely," Penny said confidently. "I'll admit, if they were high-strung performance horses, or poorly trained, I probably wouldn't leave them alone. And I'd never leave them tied if I was leaving the barn. But just stepping into the tack room, they'll be fine."

A short while later, the horses fully tacked up and ready to go, the two women led the animals from the barn and into the riding ring. Penny closed the gate behind them and carefully latched it.

"Okay, do you remember how to use a mounting block?" she asked Emma, gesturing to the hand built platform set on the side of the ring, with three steps leading up to it.

"I think I do," Emma told her hesitantly. "I remember using this thing back when George was teaching me." She led Zion over to the block before flipping the reins back over his head and grabbing the pommel of her saddle. She stuck her foot in the stirrup and threw her other leg up and over, landing hard on Zion's back. The well-behaved horse didn't move a muscle.

"Good boy," Emma crooned, leaning forward and stroking his neck. "Sorry about that," she apologized to him. "I'll be more gentle next time," she added ruefully with a glance at Penny.

"It's all about learning," Penny reassured her. "Do you remember how to ask him to walk on?" Penny asked, sticking her foot in River's stirrup and hopping up from the ground, without the aid of the mounting block. She felt a burst of pride that she was still flexible enough to pull it off.

"I just squeeze, right?" Emma asked hesitantly, her calves moving into Zion's sides a tiny bit. "Walk on, Zion," she commanded at the same time. Zion dutifully moved away from the mounting block, heading right to the edge of the ring on his accord.

"He's very well trained," Penny called out with a laugh. "Now sit up straight and loosen up your reins a little bit—he knows what he's doing!"

Sitting on River's back, Penny prompted the horse to start walking with a slight squeeze of her legs. River was responsive, but tossed her head at the command. Penny loosened her reins a little bit, accepting the request the horse was unable to voice. Sometimes, a horse and rider had to find a balance. No one was in control, but they both worked together. River settled down and moved into a smooth walk as she reached the rail, the outermost track around the ring.

"Are you ready to try trotting?" Penny called out to Emma. "We'll probably walk the whole time we're on the trail, but we want to make sure you can stay on in case we need to move more quickly."

"Let's do it!" Emma called back, enthusiasm filling her voice. Without waiting to be prompted, she squeezed her legs again, even using her mouth to make a clicking noise to Zion, indicating that he should move more quickly. He broke into a trot, throwing Emma back in the saddle briefly before she found her rhythm. She even started posting, rising and sitting in the saddle in time to the horse's gait.

"Very good!" Penny said approvingly. "Look at you go!" She pushed River into a trot as well, keeping up with Emma as they made their way around the ring.

"Are you ready to head out onto the trail?" Penny asked a moment later as they slowed the horses to a walk.

"Let's do it," Emma said confidently, using her reins to turn Zion back towards the gate.

They exited the ring, Penny leading, and walked the horses down the lane away from the farm. "So how does it feel?" Penny asked as the horses meandered in the cool shade.

"I can't believe I waited this long to try it again," Emma admitted. "I think I might become your best customer!" She giggled.

"You might be my only customer if the whole town thinks I murdered their queen bee," Penny remarked with a sigh.

"Sebastian just likes to gossip," Emma reassured her. "It wasn't you, and once the police arrest the right person, everything will be fine."

"Is there anyone else she was mean to recently?" Penny asked. "Maybe if I can give the cops another idea of where to look, they'll leave me alone."

"She was mean to everyone," Emma blurted out, gently tugging on her rein to keep Zion from eating a tree branch. "I mean, look at Lucinda. Janine bullied her their entire life about not being from a 'true founding family.'"

"Really?" Penny asked in surprise. "Lucinda made it sound like it was no big deal."

"Well, I wasn't around when they were in school together, since they're both older, but apparently Janine used to get her group of friends, who've become the Grouchy Old Ladies, together and they would taunt poor Lucinda. And once they got older, she would make sure Lucinda was excluded from all sorts of things. Janine even tried to get her fired from the hospital once," Emma informed her.

"Wow. So Lucinda must have really hated her," she realized as they crossed the main road and guided the horses down the trail on the other side.

"She claims that she doesn't have a problem with Janine," Emma stated. "But how could she not? To have the most popular girl in school, who grows up to run the town, make your life miserable? She must have hated her," Emma pointed out. "I think we need to turn here," she directed, indicating a smaller trail that branched off from the one they were on.

"You lead the way. I brought the horses, now it's your job to get us there!" Penny joked before jumping back to the topic of Janine.

"Do you think that Lucinda hated Janine enough to want her dead?" Penny asked carefully, trying not to offend her new friend.

"I really hope not," Emma admitted. "She's one of my best friends. I don't want to think that she could do that."

"Neither do I," Penny sighed.

Finally, the horses emerged from the trees, and the beach unfolded before them in the bright sunlight. They were surrounded by dunes covered in scraggly beach grass. River tried to snag a bite, but Penny gently guided her back onto the trail. Emma tugged on her reins, coaxing Zion to a halt, and Penny followed suit.

"Okay, so if we go straight ahead, that's the actual beach," Emma told Penny, pointing at the trail that wound its way through the dunes. "There probably aren't that many people on the beach. It's public, but there are no lifeguards, and we have a few shark sightings here each summer, so the tourists mostly avoid it," she explained.

"Sharks?" Penny asked in surprise. "I thought you said this was a public beach!"

"Sharks," Emma confirmed with a nod. "There are a lot of great whites in the area. It *is* a public beach, and the locals know to be smart about it. If we don't bother the sharks, and stay out of the water at dawn and dusk when they like to feed, everything is fine." She shrugged. "There are a lot of sharks in the water around Cape Cod. There's usually at least one shark attack every summer somewhere on the Cape."

"I had no idea," Penny gulped. "I guess I won't be going swimming for a while then!" she exclaimed, gazing out at the peaceful water beyond the dunes. It seemed impossible to imagine a deadly shark lurking below the surface.

"You just have to be careful," Emma assured her, shrugging. "Sharks are a part of life here on the Cape. And this spot is really popular with them. A lot of the other beaches in town are perfectly safe," she added. "There are a lot of seals in this particular area, which is what the sharks hunt."

"Anyway," Emma continued. "If we go this way," she explained, gesturing to the trail running between the dunes and the forest they had emerged from, "that takes us straight to the spot where the historical society wants to build its monument."

"Let's go to the monument site," Penny decided. "Maybe on our way back we can head down to the beach and see how crowded it is. I'd like to see how the horses do around the water."

They turned to the left, following the trail as it ran between the dunes and the forest. A drop of sweat rolled down Penny's cheek as they rode; she was glad she'd worn a baseball cap to shield her face from the hot sun.

Eventually reaching the end of the trail, Emma gestured to a small parking lot. "See, that's the only parking lot for the beach. People have to park here and walk down the trail, then go through the dunes."

"That's probably another reason it's not so popular," Penny realized. "Well, it'll be nice to have such an uncrowded beach close by."

"The monument is going to go over here," Emma pointed to the spot as she encouraged Zion to walk across the parking lot. There was a small grassy area between the parking lot and the dunes.

"If the lot does get sold, the dunes will be razed and they'll probably build summer condos," Emma explained over the loud *clip-clop* sound of the horse's hooves on the pavement. "The same developer already did it once on the other side of town."

"They can just knock down the dunes to build houses?" Penny asked in astonishment. "That can't be legal. No way!" she exclaimed, her raised voice spooking River. The horse danced to the side, her ears flicking back.

"Shh, girl, it's okay," Penny assured the horse, getting her temper under control and stroking the horse's pale gray neck. "Sorry, River," she apologized.

"If the town zoning board approves it, they can." Emma leaned back in her saddle as Zion bent his head down to graze peacefully on the small patch of grass. "And they approved the other site, so why wouldn't they do the same here?"

"That would be such a shame," Penny remarked, still absentmindedly stroking River's neck. "I hope Lisa will shut down the deal."

"Me too," Emma agreed grimly. "Do you want to go back and ride down the trail to the beach?"

"Let's do it," Penny said, urging River to walk back the way they had come. "Do you know how to neck rein, girl?" she murmured to the horse, moving her reins side to side so they touched the horses neck without pulling on the bit. River responded accordingly, turning away from the side that the rein touched her neck on. "Good girl!" Penny cried, vigorously rubbing the horse's neck.

Reaching the turn off to head towards the beach, Penny used their newly-discovered skill to turn down the trail. She continued on, checking behind her to make sure Emma had successfully made the turn as well.

A few moments later, they emerged from the dunes onto the wide, sandy beach, the ocean spilling out in front of them all the way to the horizon. Waves gently lapped at the shore, and seals frolicked in the water just beyond. "Wow," Penny breathed, stopping the horse to take in the view. A sailboat, way out to sea, tacked back and forth in the breeze, slowly crossing the wide expanse of blue ocean.

"Isn't this place gorgeous?" Emma remarked, stopping Zion next to River. "I bring the kids here all the time, since they don't like to actually swim. They just want to build sand castles," she added with a smile.

"It's amazing." Penny took it all in. "Gosh, I sure hope this place doesn't get ruined just so a few rich people can have a view."

"I agree. And if it goes to the zoning board, myself and a lot of other people, the baking club included, will be there to protest," Emma declared firmly. "Now come on," she added, urging Zion ahead. "The actual spot where Black Sam is supposed to have come ashore is a little further down."

"As much as I like to bring the kids here, this beach always creeps me out just a little bit," Emma admitted as the horses walked. "Knowing that the Whydah—Black Sam Bellamy's ship—is just offshore, with all the men who drowned when it went down."

"I hadn't really thought of it like that," Penny admitted, picturing an old sailing ship as she gazed out over the water. "It's tough to imagine, on a beautiful day like today, a storm big enough to sink a ship."

"Oh, just you wait," Emma warned with a laugh. "Winter is no joke around here. I know you're from Montana, where it gets crazy cold, so you're used to that. The temperatures don't drop too much here, but we get massive ice storms and flooding."

"Trust me, I believe you." Penny sighed, leaning back in her saddle and stretching her lower back. "I may not have been out here on the Cape, but I have been living on the east coast for a while now. I'll be ready," she declared confidently.

"It's hard to imagine that winter will ever come on such a hot day," Emma commented, giving her rein a gentle tug to keep Zion heading in the right direction.

"I agree." Penny leaned back in her saddle and tilted her head back in the warm sunlight. "I hope it never comes." she added wistfully.

They meandered down the beach, the horses taking their time navigating through the sand. Suddenly, Penny spotted a deep hole in the sand, and another, and another. "Stop!" she cried out to Emma, who was ahead of them. "Stop moving!" she repeated. Zion jerked to a halt as Emma twisted in the saddle.

"What is it?" she asked, confusion spreading over her face.

"All these holes," Penny called out, gesturing to the ground. "If one of the horses steps in one, they could break a leg," she exclaimed, dismounting. She landed on the soft sand, sending up a little cloud of dust. "Stay right where you are," she directed Emma. "I'm going to lead River back up the beach a little and then I'll come back and lead Zion," she explained.

"Okay," Emma replied nervously, gazing at the holes surrounding them. Penny grabbed River's reins and carefully led the horse back away from the holes, leaving her a safe distance down the beach. "I hope you know how to ground tie, girl," she said, dropping the reins on the ground. There was nothing nearby for Penny to tie the horse to. "I'll be right back," she told the horse, who was now grazing peacefully on the beach grass.

Penny headed back to Emma and Zion, still standing exactly where they had stopped. "Come on, boy," Penny cajoled, using one hand to pull back on the reins under the horse's chin as she used the other to push on his chest, in the same direction. "It's safer to get him to back straight up, rather than try to turn around," she explained to Emma, still perched in the saddle, as she guided the horse backward. "Good boy," she soothed Zion.

Finally, they reached the edge of the patch where the holes were. "Good boy," she said again, allowing him to turn back around. She headed back to River, who was still standing exactly where Penny had left her. "Good girl," Penny told the mare reassuringly as she approached, grabbing the reins and flipping them back over the horse's head. She stuck her foot in the stirrup and hopped back into the saddle.

"Thank you," Emma shuddered, her voice still nervous. "Why would someone dig all those holes?"

"Is that where Bellamy is supposed to have come ashore?" Penny asked. "Maybe someone really is looking for his treasure again."

"That is the spot," Emma replied. "But why would they dig up the whole beach like that? It's dangerous, and not just for the horses," she added. "A person could break their leg in one of those holes, too."

"I have no idea," Penny admitted as they turned onto the trail that led back to the farm. "No idea at all."

"It might be another one of those treasure hunting groups," Emma suggested. "We get one every few years. Out-of-towners who think they've found some clue to Black Sam's treasure, and they come here to dig it up. Of course, no one has ever found anything."

"Out-of-towners?" Penny asked. "Really? People from other towns know about this legend?"

"Oh, everyone on Cape Cod knows it!" Emma scoffed. "It's taught in all the schools. It's the only thing that makes Bellamy Cove notable," she pointed out.

"Well, whoever it was, I sure hope they're done trying to destroy this lovely beach," Penny sighed as they headed back through the woods.

✳ ✳ ✳

Chapter 9

_____After untacking the horses and letting them out into the pasture, Emma headed back to town, leaving Penny alone on the farm. Joe was nowhere to be seen—it was his day off, and his truck had disappeared early that morning.

Penny headed into the house to grab the freshly washed horse blankets she had tackled earlier in the week. Neatly folded, she stacked them in the tack room. "I'll need to get a blanket hanger before winter comes," she mused to the gray barn cat, Stilton, that had emerged from Joe's apartment. "Unless George Collins had some up in the hay loft?"

Penny headed up the barn stairs to the loft. One side of the upper level was Joe's apartment, and the other was a hay loft, where all the hay for the horses was stored, along with miscellaneous equipment and supplies. After the hay had been delivered shortly after her arrival, she hadn't stepped foot in the loft.

Penny turned the corner into the loft and gasped in surprise. There was white paint thrown all over the hay, and nearly every inch of it was covered. "Oh no," Penny groaned. This hay was supposed to last until the winter - and had cost a pretty penny.

Penny started moving the bales of hay, struggling to lift them in the cramped loft. *Maybe the hay underneath is fine*, she thought hopefully. But no, every single bale had paint thrown onto it. The vandal had been very thorough. Penny kicked something as she struggled to replace the bale she had lifted; an empty paint can. She bent down to examine it and discovered that the vandal had used the leftover paint she and Joe had painted the barn with earlier in the week.

"Why would someone do this?" Penny asked out loud in the empty space. The gray barn cat had followed her up the stairs and sat at her feet, looking just as upset as she felt. Penny knelt down and gave it a scratch under the chin as she gazed at the destruction.

"What are we going to do, Stilton?" With a sigh, she stood back up. "I guess it's time for another trip to the farm store. We'll need more hay as soon as we can get it. I'll deal with this when I get back," she decided, gazing at the ruined hay. She headed back downstairs and climbed into her Jeep, passing the horses grazing peacefully in the field.

On the other side of town, Penny made her way to Jack's Farm Emporium, parking in the small lot. "Hi, Jack," she called out to the older man behind the counter.

"Back already?" he asked, coming around the counter. "You'll be my best customer pretty soon!

You'll have all those cranberry guys beat in no time," he continued with a smile, referencing the many cranberry farms located on Cape Cod.

"I might just," Penny scoffed. "I need to place another order for hay. Someone threw paint all over the stuff I had delivered last week," she admitted grimly.

Jack's expression changed from laughter to anger in a heartbeat. "Someone destroyed all that hay? That was enough to feed those horses for at least a month, if not two! Who was it?"

"I have no idea," Penny admitted. "But I also want to buy a few locks while I'm here, so I can lock the doors to the hayloft and the tack room," she added. "And one for Joe's apartment too. I'm not letting this vandal destroy anything else."

"Of course," Jack assured her, crossing the store and grabbing a few locks off a shelf. "And I'll make sure that hay is delivered, ASAP. Is there anything else?" he asked, laying the locks on the counter.

"Do you carry blanket chains, for horse blankets?" Penny asked. "The kind that hangs across a stall door."

"I don't have them in stock, but I'd be happy to order some for you," Jack informed her. "I can have them here in a week or two. I'll give you a call when they arrive. How many?"

"Six, please," Penny decided. "I may as well get one for every stall while I'm at it, even if I don't need them yet. How much for the locks?"

"They're on me," Jack told her kindly. "I know you haven't had a very warm welcome to Bellamy Cove, the least I can do is help you avoid any more trouble."

"Thank you," Penny said gratefully. "If you'd ever like to take a trail ride, please feel free to come by the farm," she offered.

"Thanks, dear. Now get on home and get those installed. I don't want to have to sell you any more hay—not for a while, at least!" Jack instructed with a smile.

Penny thanked him again and headed back out to the Jeep, tossing the locks on the passenger seat next to her.

As she passed back through town, Penny couldn't help but stomp on the brake pedal in surprise. A large group of people had gathered on the town green, surrounding the pavilion. *Where did they all come from?* She wondered as she slowed the Jeep to a stop. *This place was empty just half an hour ago.* Rolling down the windows, Penny could just hear what they were chanting. "No sale, no sale," echoed through the small town.

Penny quickly parked her car and climbed out, crossing the green to see what all the fuss was about. She spotted Lucinda on the outskirts of the crowd and joined her.

"What's going on?" Penny asked, bewildered. "Where did all these people come from? They weren't here when I came through town twenty minutes ago."

"They're protesting the sale of the Hallett land," Lucinda explained. "They must have planned it; all these people just showed up out of nowhere with signs." She pointed to one of the men up front, who seemed particularly passionate. "That's Mike Harrie, the president of the Bellamy Cove Historical Society. He's been against the sale ever since the rumors started a few months ago."

"Really," Penny remarked, thinking. "Do you think he was upset enough about it to kill Janine?"

"I'm not sure, but I know he was really angry," Lucinda admitted, running a hand through her short grey curls. "The two of them got into a shouting match at a town meeting last month."

"And the cops haven't thought to talk to him at all?" Penny exclaimed indignantly. "He's got a much better motive than I do! Even you have a better motive than I do!" she blurted, covering her mouth as soon as she realized what had slipped out.

"That's not to say…I don't mean that you did it…" she trailed off as a blush bright enough to match her hair spread over Penny's face. "I just mean that I didn't have a very good motive. I didn't know the lady at all," she stuttered, hands still hiding her mouth, hoping to draw the words back in.

"I know what you meant," Lucinda countered, her voice still soothing. "And I'm not offended. You're right, I had just as much opportunity as you, and she did spend her entire life hating me," she added with a shrug.

"But…you didn't do it, right?" Penny asked hesitantly. They were still surrounded by protestors, their chanting aimed at no one in particular.

"I most certainly did not do it," Lucinda declared firmly. "I was next to you the entire time. Did you ever see me adding something to her pie?"

"No," Penny admitted. "And besides, you would have had no way of knowing that it was the right piece of pie," she realized. "I didn't mean to accuse you, though."

"I know you didn't, dear," Lucinda said, squeezing her hand. "I'm going to go now, though. I have no interest in standing around watching these troublemakers." With that, Lucinda left, disappearing into the crowd.

Now standing alone, Penny wove her way through the crowd, moving up to the front where Mike Harrie was standing, waving a sign crudely painted to read: "Keep Our Town's History!" He was chanting the same slogan as the rest of the crowd, slightly off-beat.

"Excuse me," Penny began, arriving next to him. "I'm Penny Bowden," she introduced herself, smiling politely.

"I know who you are," Mike scoffed, glancing at her before going back to his vigorous protesting.

"Okay," Penny continued, taking a deep breath. "Well, I was wondering if you were...at the bake-off," she asked, blurting the question out in a rush. "I didn't see you there," she explained belatedly.

"I don't think that is any of your business, young lady," he interrupted rudely, turning away from her. "From what I hear, you've got enough to worry about already," he added as he walked away.

Whoa, Penny thought, silently staring after him. *He certainly seemed defensive.* She was moving back through the crowd, ready to head home, when the feedback from a megaphone caught her attention. Turning back around, Penny was surprised to see that Lisa Hallett had taken the stage in the pavilion, facing the crowd. She was escorted by a young woman and two police officers. *Officer Calhoun and Officer Dawes.* The same officers who had been at the crime scene.

"Hello, everyone," Lisa announced. She was dressed in all black, with a long, flowing silk robe draped over her shoulders. A black sun hat was perched atop her dark hair. "I'm so glad to see the passion you all hold for our town's history!" she continued in a dramatic tone, wincing as the feedback interrupted her.

"I'm here for one reason today!" she cried into the megaphone. "And that, my dear townspeople, is to tell you all that you are free to go home, because the Hallett beach will not be sold!"

The crowd erupted into cheers.

"As it has always been," Lisa continued, "the land will be free for the townspeople to use. The dunes will remain untouched, and the historical society will be able to construct its marker, commemorating the legend of Black Sam Bellamy!" she exclaimed, her free hand rising into the air. "I will be meeting with Mike, the lovely president of the historical society, so we can determine how best to achieve this goal. Thank you all!" she finished, stepping back.

Lisa handed the megaphone to the young woman at her side and descended from the pavilion. She hurried across the green, giving the protestors a distracted wave, and climbed into a black sedan. The young woman scrambled to join her, barely closing the car door before it sped away. The two police officers descended from the pavilion more slowly.

"Ms. Bowden!" Officer Calhoun called out.

Penny hesitated for a second. "Yes?" she called back as the two men approached.

"I'd like to inform that you are no longer considered a suspect in the murder of Janine Hallett," Officer Calhoun informed her. "We have determined that you had neither a motive nor access to the poison," he added, less formally.

"That's what I've been telling you all along!" Penny cried out indignantly. She paused for a second, taking a deep breath and getting her temper under control. "I do appreciate you telling me, though," she continued, keeping her tone even. "Does that mean you have another suspect?"

"We are not able to comment on the investigation at this time," Officer Dawes broke in. "Thank you for your time, Ms. Bowden," he said formally before the two officers started to step away.

"Wait!" Penny called after them. The officers turned back to face her expectantly. "I'm sorry, this is unrelated, but someone broke into my hay loft and threw a can of paint all over my hay. They vandalized it," she told the officers.

Officer Calhoun took a step closer. "Vandalism, Ms. Bowden?" he asked her, raising an eyebrow. "That's a strong word. Are you sure the paint didn't just fall over?"

"Of course I'm sure," Penny insisted. "There was only one leftover can, and it was sealed tightly. Someone picked it up and poured it across all the hay in the loft. A dozen bales, at least."

"Mmhmm," Officer Calhoun hummed, nodding. "I'm sure. Well, let us know if anything else happens," he added doubtfully, turning away again. This time Penny let them leave, shaking her head.

Those two are not very good at their jobs. Or maybe they just hate outsiders, the same as everyone else seems to.

"That was so weird," Penny muttered to herself as she watched them climb back into their cruiser.

"Lisa's speech?" a voice asked from behind her, causing Penny to jump. She spun around to see Caroline, barely holding back a laugh.

"You scared me!" Penny gasped, holding a hand to her heart.

"Sorry, I couldn't help myself!" Caroline chortled. "What were the officers saying to you?"

"They were telling me that I'm no longer a suspect in Janine's murder!" Penny told Caroline triumphantly. "They must have seen me watching Lisa's speech."

"Congratulations!" Caroline exclaimed, giving Penny a hug. "That must be a weight off your shoulders, huh? Did they say who they suspect now?"

"They didn't say a word about any other suspects," Penny told her. "And I do feel a lot better. I mean, obviously I didn't do it, but it's a relief to have the police realize that," she confessed. "Were you here for Lisa's speech?" she asked, changing the subject. "It was kind of bizarre, wasn't it? The way she just popped up out of nowhere, and then vanished after she made her announcement."

"I can't believe that there was a protest at all," Caroline confessed. "I mean, Mike is certainly passionate about preserving the history of this town, but organizing a protest over a land sale is a little much," she added with a half-smile. "Sometimes, he can get carried away. Honestly, I think he would do anything if he thought it would save a piece of our history," she continued, a strange note in her voice.

"Do you know him well?" Penny asked eagerly. *Would Mike Harrie go so far as to kill to save a piece of Bellamy Cove History?*

"I do some volunteer work for the historical society, so I've worked with him a little. But I don't know him well. I mostly spend my volunteer time sorting through old documents," Caroline explained. "Why do you ask?"

"I'm just trying to learn as much as I can about the people who live here," Penny explained quickly. "If I get to know them, maybe they'll finally stop accusing me of murder!" she joked as the two women began to walk together back towards their cars.

"So what brings you to town today?" Caroline asked as they approached the municipal lot next to the town green. "I'd have thought you'd be spending the next few weeks holed up on the farm, getting it ready for customers."

"You'll never believe it!" Penny cried, her mind shooting straight back to the vandalism. She'd let the protest distract her, but now she was fired up again. "Someone vandalized my hay! At least a month's worth. They threw paint all over it!"

Caroline held up a hand to cut her off. "Someone vandalized your hay? What do you mean?"

"Well," Penny told her as they stopped walking, halfway across the green. "Someone sabotaged my hay. They threw paint all over it. I was at the store ordering more, and buying locks for the hayloft and the tack room," she explained.

"When I came back through town I saw the protest, so I stopped."

"Do you have any idea who did it?" Caroline asked, a note of urgency in her voice. "Because that's destruction of property. If you know who did it, they can go to jail. And I can help you sue them for the cost of the hay."

"I have no idea," Penny admitted. "I talked to the officers about it, just now, but they didn't seem concerned."

"You should go down to the station and file a police report, anyway," Caroline advised. "Get it on record in case you do find out who did it, or it happens again. This is usually such a quiet, sleepy town," Caroline continued, shaking her head. "Nothing ever happens here. And now, this week alone we've had a murder, vandalism, and a protest!"

"I hope I didn't bring the big city with me," Penny joked, crossing her fingers. As the two women resumed walking across the green, she changed the subject. "Do you have any idea where I could see the pictures that photographer was taking the other day, at the bake-off?" she asked Caroline. "I'd like to see if someone was there."

"Who?" Caroline asked in surprise, raising an eyebrow.

"Well," Penny began hesitantly, "Mike Harrie. Lucinda let me know that he had quite a grudge against Janine Hallett," she explained. "And if he was there, maybe he was the one who slipped poison into her pie. I guess I'm not a suspect any more, but I'd still like to get to the bottom of this. Maybe I can get the fine citizens of Bellamy Cove to stop harassing me."

"Doing a little detective work, huh?" Caroline asked with a smile. "Don't worry, the police here will get to the bottom of it, I promise. But in the meantime, if you want to take a look at the pictures, I'm sure that Sarah has posted them online by now."

"Sarah was the photographer?" Penny asked, still trying to learn the names of all her new neighbors.

"Yes, sorry," Caroline apologized, shaking her head at her lapse in memory as they arrived at the parked cars. "Sarah Lachlan is the town photographer. Well, she's really a teacher at the elementary school, but she does the photos for all the town events, too. She usually posts them on the town website within a day or two."

"Thank you," Penny said gratefully. "I guess I'm off to do some investigating!" she added with a smile before she climbed into her Jeep and headed for home.

✳ ✳ ✳

Chapter 10

Back at the farm, Penny ran into Joe, who was just arriving himself. She parked the Jeep next to his old, gray truck and climbed out. "Hi, Joe!" she called to him.

"Penny," he greeted her with a nod. "What's all that?" He gestured to the locks Penny had grabbed from the passenger seat.

"We had a bit of excitement while Emma and I were out on our trail ride," she explained. "Someone broke in and threw the leftover paint all over the hay in the hayloft."

"Oh, no!" Joe exclaimed, looking concerned. "Is it totally ruined?" he asked, taking the locks out of Penny's hands.

"It sure is," Penny said regretfully. "I just came from the farm store. Jack is sending out another delivery for us, sometime next week. Luckily, the bales that you'd already pulled down from the loft didn't get damaged, so the horses will have enough to eat until the delivery. I also bought locks for the hay loft, the tack room, and your apartment."

"I'll get them installed right away," Joe promised, raking his hand through his short gray hair. "I can't believe I wasn't here. I'm sorry, Penny."

"No, it's not your fault." Penny protested. "We'll just have to make sure one of us is always here until we figure out who did it. And I'll install the locks myself - it's your day off!"

"I'd rather get it done sooner than later, if someone is really running around destroying things," he countered. "It'll hardly take any time at all," Joe assured her over his shoulder as he headed into the barn, ignoring her protests. "And I'll take care of the ruined hay tomorrow."

"Thank you!" Penny called out as he disappeared into the building. She headed towards the house, stopping in her tracks when she saw what had been done to the picture window next to the front door. "Joe!" she shouted, her voice strangled.

He hurried out of the barn, slowing down when he saw what had caught Penny's attention. Using the same white paint that had been splattered all over the hay, someone had painted the word "MURDERER" in giant, white letters across the glass of the picture window in the living room.

"Oh no," Penny gasped. "Does someone really think I committed murder? I can't believe this," she groaned. "They destroyed my hay to drive me out of town. Someone is trying to drive me away because they think I killed Janine Hallett."

"I'll have it cleaned off in a jiff, Penny," Joe promised, hurrying back to the barn. "You just go inside and carry on. It'll be like it never happened," he said firmly.

Penny stayed where she was, staring at the word. *The police just cleared me! What do I have to do to prove to these people that I'm not a murderer?*

Joe returned, carrying a bucket full of water and a brush. "I'll take care of it," he promised her again. "Go inside and close the curtains."

"I didn't do it, Joe. The police just told me I'm no longer a suspect, barely half an hour ago!" she cried indignantly. "What, do they have to make an announcement or something?" she continued, spite creeping into her voice.

"People here are just a little wary of newcomers," Joe reminded her. "They'll come around, especially once the murder is solved and they know you didn't do it. Go on inside, and let me take care of this."

Reluctantly, Penny stepped inside, stopping to pet Cheddar, who seemed to have taken up residence in her living room. "I'm not feeding you, you know," she told him. "You still have to earn your keep by catching mice out in the barn." The cat purred, seemingly in agreement.

Penny stepped to the window and pulled the curtains closed. She could still hear Joe cleaning, but at least she didn't have to look at that awful word.

"Who would do that? Who even *could have* done that?" Penny asked Cheddar, who was picking his way across the living room. "They must have snuck onto the property while I was out with Emma. I never even glanced at the house before I went into town," she sighed.

Trying to avoid thinking about it, Penny pulled out her laptop and booted it up, settling into her armchair. The cat came over and sat on the arm, eventually lying down along it. "If the only way for people to stop harassing me is to catch the real killer, then that's what I'm going to do," she told him. He leaned over and rubbed his face against her arm, seemingly in approval.

Once the computer was ready, Penny quickly navigated to the town's website. There was a link right on the home page: See the Pictures From the Annual Bake-Off! It made no mention of the fact that a woman had been murdered at the event.

A moment later, Penny was browsing through the pictures, carefully scanning for any sign of Mike Harrie. "Nothing, nothing, nothing," she muttered to herself as she clicked through the pictures. There weren't that many; clearly, Sarah the photographer had stopped shooting once Janine had collapsed. Penny did notice that one of the last pictures showed Janine, standing alone, holding the plate of pie in one hand and a fork in another. There was one bite taken out of the piece of pie. *This must have been just before she collapsed.* It was a beautiful shot of Janine, the sun lighting up her face as she laughed at something out of the frame.

As she gazed at the image, Penny suddenly realized that something was taking place in the background of the shot. Looking more closely, she saw that someone was exiting the office of Dr. Perry, located on the edge of the town green. *Mike Harrie!*

Penny triumphantly used the browser to zoom in. It was definitely him. "But was he in there the whole time?" she asked the orange cat still sitting next to her. "Or did he poison her pie and quickly go to the doctor's office so he would have an alibi?"

Penny closed the browser. "Only one way to find out," she told the cat, setting the laptop aside. She headed back out to the yard, surprised to see that the sun had fallen halfway to the horizon. Joe had finished his work at the window, making it seem like nothing had happened.

Hopping into the Jeep, Penny headed back into town, parking in the same spot she had vacated just an hour earlier. She hurried across the town green and into the office of Dr. Perry, surprising his receptionist, who seemed like she was about to leave for the day.

"Hello!" Penny greeted her enthusiastically. "I have a question for you…" she paused, at a loss as to how to proceed. *She won't just tell me about another patient*, Penny realized.

"You're that girl who bought the old Collins place, right?" the receptionist asked in a kindly tone. "Penelope," she remembered.

"Penny, actually. And yes, I am. It's nice to meet you!" she added with a big smile, pushing her hair back.

"What can I help you with, Penny?" the woman asked, sitting back down in her chair.

"I, uh, was wondering, about an appointment, the other day. Would you mind checking to see if I had an appointment at eleven in the morning on the day of the bake-off?"

"You don't remember if you had an appointment?" the receptionist, whose nameplate read Laura, asked skeptically.

"I don't," Penny told her, trying to make her voice sound regretful. "Would you be able to find out for me?"

"Well, I certainly don't remember you coming in," Laura huffed, setting her purse down on the ground. "But I'll check," she conceded reluctantly, flipping through the pages of the appointment book on the desk in front of her.

"Thank you," Penny said gratefully, inching closer to the counter. Laura landed on the correct page and slid her finger down, stopping at the spot labeled "11." The name Michael Harrie was written on the line.

"No, dear, you didn't have an appointment," Laura told Penny, her voice now full of derision. "Would you like me to make you one? Dr. Perry would probably be very interested in these memory lapses," she added.

"I'm all set. Thank you!" Penny said quickly, turning on her heel and leaving the office. *I snooped!* she thought triumphantly as she stepped back into the humid air outside. She smiled to herself, practically beaming as she made her way back to the Jeep.

Chapter 11

The next morning, Penny was up bright and early. "I think it's time I paid my condolences to Lisa Hallett," she told Cheddar as she got dressed for the day. He had laid claim to the bedroom, sprawled out over the unused half of Penny's bed. "And maybe I'll be able to find something out about who would want Janine dead while I'm there."

Cheddar stared back at her. "I'll take that as an agreement," Penny told him. She quickly dressed, picking out a dark navy dress and a pair of flats. She tied her bright red hair back into a neat bun, pulling down a few pieces to frame her face.

Penny headed out to the barn, stopping to greet the horses, who had just been turned out to the pasture. "Morning, Joe!" she called out as she stepped into the barn.

Joe emerged from one of the stalls, pitchfork in hand. "Good morning, Penny. You look nice," he added, almost in surprise.

"Thank you," Penny said graciously. "I wanted to ask you a question. Do you know where the Hallett estate is? After everything that happened at the bake-off, I'd like to pay my respects to Lisa," she explained.

Joe nodded approvingly. "Sure do. It's just down the road. Their set up makes this place look like nothing. They breed dressage horses over there, and have tennis courts, pools, the whole nine yards."

"They breed dressage horses?" Penny asked in surprise. " I had no idea," she confessed. "I thought we were the only riding operation in town."

"Sure do," Joe confirmed. "They don't offer lessons or anything like that, though. It's all about the breeding operation. They've turned out a few Olympians over at Hallett Farms," he informed her. "Anyway, if you just turn left on the main road, away from town, you'll see the road to their place about a mile down. It's on the beach side of the road—their dressage ring has a million dollar view of the Atlantic," he added with a smile.

"Thanks," Penny remarked gratefully. "I had no idea that it was, well, an estate," she admitted, suddenly feeling nervous.

"You'll be fine. I'm friends with their barn manager, been there plenty of times. It's a nice place."

"Well, wish me luck," Penny joked as she left the barn and climbed into the Jeep. She set off, making her way out to the main road and quickly finding the road to the Hallett estate, marked "Private." She turned down it, watching in awe as the trees faded away to carefully manicured grass, with miles of fencing dividing it into neat paddocks. Graceful, muscular horses grazed on the green grass, the bright blue ocean spreading out behind them. A large, pale yellow barn sat ahead, with a covered riding ring on one side and an open-air one on the other. At the end of the drive sat the house, a huge stone mansion looming over the rest of the property, with long wings sprawling out to either side.

"Wow," Penny muttered to herself as she parked. She watched as an exercise rider put a tall palomino stallion through its paces, the horse's long legs flashing out in front of him as he moved across the ring.

She crossed the drive and leaned against the fence around the riding ring, wishing that she had that much skill. *I can ride, but I can't make it look like poetry.*

"Hello," rang out a voice from behind her, cool and collected. Penny turned around and saw a young woman with brown hair, on the shorter side. She was wearing a very sensible skirt with a dark blouse. It was the same woman who had accompanied Lisa at the protest the day before.

"Hi," Penny responded, putting on a smile. "I'm Penny Bowden. I came by to offer my condolences to Lisa," she explained.

The woman's face relaxed. "Oh, of course. The new owner at Seahorse Stables. I'm Martha, Lisa's personal assistant. Why don't you come inside?"

Penny stepped away from the fence, shooting one more glance at the beautiful horse behind her. She followed Martha into the house, through the huge wooden door and into the foyer. The walls soared up around her, oak paneled with massive oil paintings.

"Wow," Penny sighed, marveling at her surroundings.

"Pretty impressive, huh?" Martha remarked, glancing over at her.

Penny smiled. "It's gorgeous. The Hallett's are a lucky family."

Martha returned the smile. "They sure are. Wait here a moment, I'll go let Lisa know that you're here."

Left alone, Penny couldn't resist peering down one of the hallways that branched off from the foyer. It seemed to stretch for miles, with the same paneling as the foyer. The hallway had more doors than Penny could count.

"Welcome to Hallett House," came Lisa Hallett's voice, cool but gracious. She had emerged from the hallway on the other side of the foyer. Penny blushed a little at having been caught.

"Your house is beautiful," she told the other woman, stepping back into the foyer. "I'm Penny

Bowden. I just moved to town. I wanted to come by and introduce myself, and tell you how sorry I am about what happened to your mother."

Lisa smiled politely. "I know who you are. Thank you for coming by, but I'm doing just fine. My mother wasn't the warmest woman," she admitted to Penny. "She cared more about looking good to others than actually *being* good."

Penny hesitated, not quite sure how to respond. "I...I'm sure she was doing what she thought was best," she stuttered.

"I'm sorry for oversharing," Lisa sighed, shaking her head. "I shouldn't burden you with my woes. Would you like a tour of the house?" she offered, pasting a polite smile on her elegant face.

"I'd love one," Penny responded quickly, hoping to forget their awkward exchange. "The house must have an incredible view out over the ocean."

They set off together, Lisa reciting a tour she'd clearly given many times before. "We'll start with the east wing. This is where the formal rooms are. The library, the dining room, the game room," she listed off.

"The formal rooms?" Penny wondered.

"The rooms used for entertaining," Lisa explained. "Above these are the guest bedrooms.

The other wing, the west wing, is for the family. We each have a suite on the second floor and a study on the first."

They reached the end of the hall. "And here's the music room," Lisa continued, gesturing through a doorway to a room packed with instruments. On the other side stood a piano, gleaming in the warm light thrown off by a stained glass chandelier.

"Mother always made us take music lessons when we were younger, but it didn't stick," Lisa told her. "The room doesn't get much use."

"Us?" Penny inquired, turning to the other woman.

"My brother," Lisa explained. "He's a few years younger than me. He left Bellamy Cove when he was a teenager and has spent the last decade backpacking around the world. He won't take a cent from us," she added. "Idiot."

The two women exchanged a smile. "Let's head to the east wing," Lisa directed.

They returned to the foyer and started down the opposite hallway. "Like I said, this is where our studies are," Lisa explained. "I've never gotten much use out of mine, but I suppose I will now that I have to take over the family business." She didn't look thrilled at the prospect.

Lisa ignored most of the doors, taking Penny straight to the end of the hallway. "This is the conservatory." She pushed open a door.

Penny couldn't help but gasp as she looked out over the room. It was enclosed entirely in glass, with a view sweeping out over the Atlantic. The room itself was packed with blossoming plants, their bright flowers sparkling against the deep green of their leaves.

"My grandmother loved to garden," Lisa explained, smiling at Penny's reaction. "So my grandfather built this for her. She spent her life stocking it with every plant she came across. Since then, we've always employed a gardener to take care of everything."

"Fantastic," Penny sighed. "I would love to just sit in here and read a good book."

"I suppose," Lisa agreed, looking out over the room. "I don't spend much time here." She stepped back out of the room, gesturing to Penny to follow.

"Did your mother have a study?" Penny asked, trying to make her voice sound innocent.

"She did." Lisa stepped over to one of the doors and swung it open. "This was where she spent most of her time."

There were bookcases on one side of the room, made out of deep red mahogany, and a huge desk in the center. On the other side, two neat armchairs were positioned in front of a stone fireplace, a small table with a tea tray in between them. A large, framed image of family crest, with a rearing horse silhouetted against a blue background hung next to the fireplace. Underneath, in an elaborate, scrolling font, read the words: "Bred for Success."

The wall behind the desk was made up of huge, floor-to-ceiling windows, showing the same impressive view Penny had seen in the conservatory. There was a plant on a stand in the corner, it's leaves drooping from thirst.

"Lisa?" Martha, the assistant who had greeted Penny, stepping into the doorway. "The funeral home is on the phone. They have a few questions for you."

"Thank you," Lisa smiled at Martha. "Penny, I'll be a few minutes. You're welcome to wait in my study and we can continue the tour. Martha, will you show Penny to my study?" she requested. Penny held back a smile - *finally, a chance to snoop!*

Martha smiled graciously, gesturing for Penny to follow her. She led the way to another room, a few doors down the hall. "Make yourself comfortable," she directed. "Lisa will be back shortly."

This room was smaller than Janine's, without the view. It was also lined with bookcases, but Lisa's were nearly empty. There was a television instead of a fireplace, and an exercise bike in the corner.

"Thank you, Martha," Penny told the young woman. She smiled again and left, not saying a word. *Not a talkative one, then.*

Penny hesitated, waiting for the sound of Martha's footprints to fade down the hallway. When she thought the coast was clear, she hesitantly poked her head out into the hallway. *Empty. Perfect!*

She stepped out of Lisa's study, wincing as a floorboard creaked under her foot. Trying to keep her steps light, she hurried down the hallway and slipped back into Janine's study. She headed directly to the desk, and sat down at the desk, her back facing the windows and the incredible view, and slid open one of the drawers. She thumbed through the file folders—nothing unusual. Bills, competitions, horse sales. Everything was in order—all the bills paid, no outstanding invoices, nothing. There was a half-empty glass of water on the desk, a remnant of Janine's last day. Penny tried not to pay too much attention to it.

Penny moved on to the bookshelves, trying to hurry before Lisa finished up her phone call. These were packed with all sorts of volumes, from gardening books, to horse breeding, to baking. Penny ran her fingers along the books, looking for anything out of place. *I really thought this would be easier.*

Finally, something caught her eye. A small volume, tucked in the bottom shelf. The spine was unlabeled, and it was plain. The volume looked much older than anything on the shelf. Penny carefully slid it out and carried it to the desk. It wasn't large, but it was thick. There had been something embossed on the front, long ago, but it was difficult to read now.

Penny carefully flipped open the cover and was surprised to discover she was holding a Bible. On the inside cover, a family tree had carefully been traced. The tree began with Sam and Mary Hallett, and had been expanded with each subsequent generation, ending with a pair of siblings, Lisa and Mark Hallett. The family tree was barely able to fit onto the inside of the cover, the handwriting growing smaller as each generation was squeezed in.

"Amazing," Penny breathed, skimming over the names. Sam and Mary had three children, who had each married and had children of their own. She recognized several other founding family names mixed in as well as the generations grew larger.

Penny carefully tucked the Bible into her purse—this would need more time. She glanced around the study, but didn't see anything else of interest. *I'd better get back to Lisa's study.* Before she left the room, she picked up the half-drunk glass of water from Janine's desk and tilted it into the potted plant. *I hope someone finds you soon.*

She slipped out of Janine's study and hurried back down the hallway to Lisa's, slipping inside and sitting down. She breathed out a sigh of relief and was almost immediately interrupted by Lisa's return.

"Sorry, I hope you weren't too bored," she apologized politely. "Ready to continue with the tour? I'm sure you'd like to see the barn."

Penny grinned, her first real smile since she'd arrived. "I'd love to," she responded, trying to push down the guilt she was feeling over swiping the Hallett family Bible.

Lisa will never know it's gone, Penny reasoned with herself. *I'll find a way to return it. I'll bring over some flowers or something tomorrow.*

The two women returned to the foyer, stepping out through the heavy door into the bright sunlight. Lisa led the way across the drive, returning to the riding ring where the same palomino horse and rider were working.

"Beautiful, aren't they?" Lisa commented, nodding at the pair.

"That horse is amazing," Penny told her.

"I was talking about the rider," Lisa corrected in a conspiratorial tone, turning to wink at Penny. It was the first bit of fire Penny had seen from the other woman—she was glad to see some personality break through Lisa's grief.

Penny returned her smile, even if she blushed a bit as she did so. "They're both beautiful," she agreed.

Martha emerged from the house, coming after them. "Lisa!" she called out.

"What is it?" Lisa called back, not taking her gaze from the horse and rider.

"You have another call. This one is from the lawyer," Martha explained as she reached them.

"Why don't I get out of your hair?" Penny suggested, smiling at the other woman. "I can only imagine how busy you must be. We can finish the tour another time."

"Well, thank you very much for coming by. It was nice to meet you," Lisa said graciously.

"Thanks for having me. I'm sure I'll see you soon," Penny said, stepping away from them and returning to her car. She clutched her purse closed to her body, still feeling guilty about the stolen cargo inside.

She climbed into the car, breathing another sigh of relief. "I'll come back tomorrow and say it's to finish the tour. I'll just leave the Bible somewhere in the house, they'll assume it was misplaced," she reasoned with herself. "Something is strange about that Bible, and I'm going to get to the bottom of it."

Filled with resolve—and a fair amount of guilt—she started the Jeep and headed back to Seashore Stables.

She pulled into the yard and parked next to the house, happy to see that Joe had taken all the paint-covered hay out of the loft. He had it neatly piled on a tarp.

"Thanks, Joe," Penny called gratefully as she climbed out of the Jeep. "I really appreciate it."

"Of course, ma'am," he replied, not stopping his work as he loaded the hay from the tarp into his truck. "I'm going to take all this to the dump," he explained breathlessly as he slung a bale into the bed of the truck.

"Hold on one second," Penny requested, pulling out her cell phone. "I want to take some pictures. Caroline told me that if we ever find out who did it, she can help me sue them for the cost of the hay," she explained as she snapped a few photos. "That should do it," she decided, dropping her phone back into her purse. "I should have taken some before you cleaned the paint off the house, too," she sighed.

"Well, I don't know how we'll ever figure that out," Joe rasped breathlessly, resuming his task. "It's not like there was any evidence or anything. Just an empty paint can," he continued, shrugging as he bent to lift another bale.

"I'll get to the bottom of it," Penny declared confidently before heading towards the house.

Unlocking the front door, Penny stepped inside, surprised to see an envelope on the floor. "What's that?" she asked Cheddar, who was in his customary spot on the loveseat.

Penny picked up the envelope. It was totally blank on the outside, and unsealed. *Someone must have slipped it under the door*, Penny realized. Settling into her armchair, Penny tugged out the single piece of paper that was inside and unfolded it.

Get out of town – NOW! was scrawled across it in an angry, red marker. "What?" Penny gasped. *This one isn't subtle at all*, she thought to herself as she reread the message. *This is just a threat.*

"Who on earth was able to slip this under the door without Joe seeing them?" she asked Cheddar. Growing angry, Penny crumpled up the paper, preparing to toss it across the kitchen and into the garbage. Her arm raised, she paused for a second. *I should save this – it's evidence,* she realized. She carefully smoothed out the paper, tucking it into her purse. "I'm not afraid of anyone in this town," she declared to Cheddar. "No one is going to scare me away!"

Still fuming, Penny pulled the Hallett family Bible out of her purse and cracked it open, ready to do some investigating.

Chapter 12

A few hours later, Penny was startled out of her reverie by the sound of a ringing phone. "There's a landline? Who even has this number?" she asked the orange cat in surprise. He stared back at her, twitching an ear as the sound rang out again.

Penny jumped up, trying to find the phone before the caller hung up. Finally, she caught sight of a flashing light across the room and hurried to grab the phone.

"Hello!" she exclaimed into the phone as she picked it up.

"Hello," came a laughing voice, booming into the telephone. "It's Caroline. How are you?"

"Out of breath!" Penny exclaimed, gasping as she sat back down. "I had no idea there was a landline. You had me on a mad dash to find the phone."

"I'm sorry!" Caroline apologized. "I figured you knew about it. I didn't have your cell phone number, so I thought I'd call the house. I was wondering if maybe you wanted to come over for a glass of wine tonight?" she asked hopefully.

Penny grinned. "I'd love to!" *Maybe Caroline can help me figure out who wants me to leave town* so *badly*. "What time? What can I bring? Where do you live?"

"Slow down!" Caroline laughed. "Seven, nothing, and in town, just a block past Emma's house. I live above my law practice; there's a sign outside for Collins Law. Just look for that and ring the bell."

"I'll see you at seven," Penny replied excitedly. "Actually, I'm working on something that has me stumped, for the case. I'll bring it with me and maybe you can help."

"I'm happy to try!" Caroline said. "I'll see you soon."

Penny hung up the phone, setting it back in its cradle. She shimmied over to the loveseat, where Cheddar was curled up, glaring at her for interrupting his nap. "Guess who made a friend?" she asked him, scratching his chin.

"That's right - me!" she told him, humming to herself. She packed the Bible into her purse and went upstairs to change.

A short while later, Penny was in town, driving past Emma's house again. Glancing in through the window as she went by, Penny could see Emma, serving dinner to her two kids at the kitchen island. Penny smiled at the image of domestic bliss.

A block further down the road, Penny spied the Collins Law sign Caroline had mentioned. She found a spot and turned off the car, hurrying to the door. She was carrying a bottle of wine—one she had braved Sebastian Harrow at the wine store to purchase.

Penny rang the doorbell and waited impatiently, tapping her foot. A moment later, the door swung open, with Caroline standing on the other side. "Come in, come in!" she exclaimed, stepping back. Penny smiled and went inside.

"I see you faced off with Sebastian again," Caroline observed with a smile, gesturing to the wine. "Did he try to bite your head off this time?" she asked, leading the way through a darkened office to a flight of stairs at the back of the house.

"He didn't say a word," Penny told Caroline. "Just rang me up, wished me a good night. That was it!" she said, thrilled that at least one Bellamy Cove Citizen had stopped trying to accuse her of murder.

"So have you made any progress on figuring out who's sabotaging the farm?" Caroline asked as she led the way up the stairs.

"Not even a little," Penny replied. "I just don't know who would have decided they hate me so much already. It's obvious that I didn't kill Janine," she pointed out. "So why is someone so dedicated to getting me to leave town?"

"People in this town are very protective." Caroline sighed as they entered her bright and cozy apartment. There was an overstuffed sofa along one wall, with a TV opposite, and a desk at the other end of the room overlooking the street. A small kitchen was off to the side, and the bedroom next to it. Exposed beams ran the length of the room, and a brightly colored rug sat on the golden brown hardwood floor.

"I also got this creepy note today," Penny said to Caroline. "Someone must have slipped it under the front door of the house. It told me to leave town."

"Penny, that's a threat!" Caroline turned to face her. "You *need* to call the police."

"I will tomorrow," Penny promised. "You're right, things are getting a little out of hand," she admitted. "They didn't seem to care about the paint on the hay, but maybe the letter and the fact that whoever destroyed my hay also painted "murderer" on my window will convince them," she told Caroline.

"Someone painted the word "murdered" on your window?" Caroline cried out, her hands flying up into the air. "Penny! You should have called the police right away!"

"I realized that afterwards, but Joe was already cleaning it. He was almost done by the time I thought to call them," Penny confessed.

"Joe, huh?" Caroline said thoughtfully. "You know, I'm surprised he agreed to keep working for you. He was really adamant about buying the farm from me."

"He told me," Penny replied. "And to be honest, I thought things might get a little awkward. But I'm glad he stuck around; he's been a huge help. Like I said, he got that paint cleaned up the second I realized it was there."

"Anyway," Penny sighed, taking a deep breath. "Time to change the subject. This apartment is fantastic!" she marveled, impressed at how cheerful it seemed, even as they discussed such dark topics.

"I do love it up here," Caroline admitted, looking around at the cozy space. "When I first bought the building, the plan was for me to keep living at the farm with my Dad and rent out this apartment, but when I saw it I knew I had to live here. Plus, it is awfully convenient to live right above the office." She laughed. "Now take a seat! Let me get this opened up," she urged, taking the bottle of wine from Penny.

"So tell me, what's this problem you need help with?" Caroline asked as she pulled a corkscrew from a drawer in the kitchen.

Penny sat down on the overstuffed sofa. "Well," she began, pulling the Hallett family Bible out of her purse, "it's a long story." Penny quickly told Caroline all about her day, and her introduction to Hallett House.

"It's beautiful there, isn't it?" Caroline asked as she carried over two glasses of wine. "They throw a party every January for the whole town—that's the only time I've ever been to the estate. They do sleigh rides, a catered dinner, the whole shebang," she explained, sitting next to Penny on the overstuffed sofa.

"Wow. The family really is pretty generous, aren't they?" she mused, sipping from her glass.

"They've been good to this town, that's for sure," Caroline agreed. "Regardless of how unpleasant Janine was as a person, she was always doing something to help the town or the people who live here," she admitted. "Now tell me, what's the deal with this Bible?" She gestured to the book that Penny still held.

"I...borrowed it," Penny fibbed. "It's the Hallett family Bible. I think it goes all the way back to Sam and Mary Hallett," Penny explained, gently opening the book to show Caroline the family tree. "But I've been flipping through the book, and there's something strange about it. I can't quite put my finger on it."

"Well, from what I know about the Hallett family, this seems to make sense." Caroline looked over the family tree. "See how all the women keep the name Hallett, even once they get married? That's how the owner of the estate is always a Hallett, even if the daughter inherits," she explained.

"Interesting. I hadn't noticed that," Penny admitted. "I guess I assumed that Janine's husband had been the one who inherited the estate."

"Nope, it was Janine. Sometimes, the husband will change their name to Hallett, other times, he just keeps his name. But the kids are always Halletts." Caroline picked up the book and began to gently flip through it.

"Well, even so, I don't think the family tree is what's weird about it," Penny said. "I just don't know what is, though. I've never really been much for church, or Bibles."

"Well, neither was I, but my father would read to us from the Bible every Sunday, growing up," Caroline remarked, still flipping the pages. "And when we got older, we had to read to him."

Suddenly, she stopped. "The pages are out of order," Caroline exclaimed. "Look at this. See how they've been sliced along the spine, and then very carefully pasted back in? But they're in the wrong order," she said again, staring intently at the book.

"Someone cut it apart and glued it back together?" Penny asked in shock, peering at the Bible. Now that Caroline had pointed it out, she could see the nearly-imperceptible seams where the pages had been rejoined.

"Wait a second," Penny exclaimed, holding out a hand to prevent Caroline from turning the page. "Look at this - each left-hand page starts with a drop cap," she pointed out. "See how the letter that starts the page is bigger than the rest? Every single page has one," she realized, taking the book and carefully turning the pages herself. "Where does it start?"

Penny turned the pages until she reached the beginning of the reordered pages. "Here," she told Caroline, taking the book from her hands. "See? It starts with an L."

Caroline, still silent, watched as Penny carefully turned the pages.

"O...O...K," Penny read. "Look?" she asked hesitantly. "Do you think this could be about Black Sam Bellamy's treasure?" she wondered, her eyes growing bigger.

"Keep going!" Caroline urged.

"U...N...D...E...R" Penny continued. "Look under....H...O...U...S...E. Look under house! That's the message!" she exclaimed.

"Under house? Black Sam buried his treasure under that giant mansion?" Penny asked skeptically, setting down the book. "How will anyone ever find it?"

"No, no, not that house," Caroline scoffed. "The big house was built by Sam's great grandkids, and was expanded by Janine's parents. Sam and Mary Hallett lived in a two-room house that's still standing, near the edge of the estate! Come on, let's go!" She jumped to her feet.

"No, no, no," Penny protested, waving her hand. "We can't go dig up a historical site. Let's tell the police and they can check it out tomorrow," she reasoned.

"Oh, come on!" Caroline slipped on her shoes. "The house is tiny, the treasure has to be easy to find. We'll tell the police once we have it. Wouldn't that be great, to be able to show them up after they accused you of murder?" She smirked, her eyes glinting in the warm light. "Let's go! I'll drive!" Caroline headed down the stairs, with Penny reluctantly following.

Stepping outside, Penny was thrilled to see that it had started to rain. *Finally! It's been weeks since we had a good rain. Now poor Joe can stop watering the pasture every morning.*

"I hope you know this is a bad idea," Penny sighed as they drove through town. "The only reason I'm coming with you is because this treasure is somehow tied up in Janine's death."

"You think so?" Caroline asked, glancing over at Penny as she navigated past the empty town green, cloaked in darkness.

"Think about it," Penny said. "She was going to sell that land, where everyone thought the treasure was buried." Slowly, a thought formed in Penny's mind. "And then immediately after she died, in Lisa's arms, Lisa stopped the sale."

Caroline gasped. "You think Lisa did it? You think she killed her own mother so she could keep the land and find the treasure?"

"I do," Penny realized, nodding her head in the dimly-lit car.

"And to think, all along, the treasure was right there on the estate!" Caroline exclaimed, laughing.

They passed the turn off for Seashore Stables, the lights from Joe's apartment flickering through the trees. As they approached the road leading to Hallett House, Caroline switched off the headlights. "I don't want anyone to see us," she explained. "We'll have to pass by pretty close to the main house."

"Are you sure we should be doing this?" Penny asked again. "This has to be illegal," she pointed out.

"I'm a lawyer! Trust me, I've worked with the cops in this town *a lot*. As long as they come out looking pretty, which they will once we hand them the case wrapped up with a bow, they'll be thrilled with us," she added in a droll voice.

"I think this is the turn off," she continued, turning away from Hallett House and down a small, dirt road. They meandered through the pastures, eventually stopping at a tiny house, little more than a shack, built on the bluffs overlooking the ocean.

"This is where Sam and Mary Hallett lived," Caroline told Penny, climbing out of the car. Penny tucked her purse down into the footwell of the front seat and followed. The house had been built from logs, with mud smeared between them as insulation. "The door is around the other side," Caroline explained, leading the way around the house.

"Should we try the root cellar?" Penny gestured to the pair of double doors set into the ground in front of the car. "If he said the treasure is 'under the house,' wouldn't it make sense to start down there?"

Caroline smiled approvingly. "You're smarter than you look! That makes perfect sense."

The two women stepped over to the root cellar doors, each lifting one. Penny grimaced as a loud *creak* rang out into the night.

"Let's go!" Caroline whispered, carefully stepping down onto the steep set of stairs.

"Wait," Penny cautioned, handing over the tiny flashlight she kept in her purse. "Use that."

"Always prepared! You're a regular Nancy Drew," Caroline whispered with a smile. She descended down into the darkness, the tiny flashlight beam the only sign of her.

"Come on down," Caroline called in a low voice. Penny gulped and, crossing her fingers for luck, climbed down into the dark room.

"How big is it?" Penny wondered as her eyes adjusted to the darkness. Without being able to tell the difference between the pitch-black night and the walls, it seemed like the room went on forever.

"Not big," Caroline answered, waving the flashlight around. "Do you see anything unusual? Anything that could be gold, or silver?" she asked eagerly.

Penny carefully examined the room in the small amount of light thrown from the flashlight. A sliver of moonlight came in through the open door at the top of the narrow stairs.

"I don't see a thing," she said, disappointedly. "There's nothing at all down here," she added, glancing around.

"I thought there'd be, like, an old piece of furniture or a chest or something," Caroline confessed dejectedly. "And the treasure would be inside."

"Could it be buried?" Penny wondered as she spied a sunken spot in the dirt floor. "Look here. This spot is lower than the rest - like it was dug up and refilled."

"Let's start digging!" Caroline cried out, forgetting to keep her voice low.

"With what?" Penny asked, raising an eyebrow. "Do you have a shovel in your car?"

"No, but here." Caroline hurried over to the corner of the root cellar, where a small piece of scrap wood was leaning against the wall. "Use this," she urged, handing it to Penny.

"You want me to dig a hole using a two by four?" Penny asked skeptically, looking at the old piece of wood. "Aren't you going to help?"

"I'm going to hold the flashlight! Come on! Don't you want to find the treasure? The town will love us forever if we're the one that proves that Sam Hallett was really Black Sam Bellamy!" Caroline told her. "Loosen up the dirt and I'll dig with my hands."

Penny got to work, scraping away the dirt as best she could. She used the corner of the wood to loosen in, before reaching into the small hole and scooping away the dirt. Caroline quickly joined in, and soon they were both covered in dirt up to their elbows.

"This better be worth it," Caroline joked as they dug.

"I think it might be," Penny realized slowly, as her fingers scraped a wooden box. Working carefully, she loosened it while Caroline watched, a smile spreading across her face. Penny slowly prized the box from the ground, setting it down in between them.

"I can't believe it's real," she whispered in awe as she looked at the simple wooden box. "Do you think this is really it? The treasure that Black Sam buried for his descendants to find one day?"

"Open it!" Caroline commanded, ignoring the question. When Penny hesitated, she reached out and did it herself.

Caroline unlatched the lid, carefully flipping it open. Inside rested a small burlap sack, discolored with age, and a leather-bound book.

"So you managed to find it," rang out a new voice, filled with confidence.

Penny looked up in shock as Lisa Hallett carefully descended the staircase.

Caroline stood up, moving to block the treasure box from view. Penny quickly shut the lid, hoping that Lisa hadn't seen what was inside.

"Found what?" Caroline asked. "All that's in that box is an old journal. Probably Sam Hallett's farming notes or something. Nothing interesting."

"Then why are you hiding it?" Lisa demanded, stepping into the room. "And why are you trespassing on my property in the middle of the night, anyway?" she asked, crossing her arms.

"I'm sorry, Lisa," Penny apologized. "I...well, I happened to see a clue that led us here," she explained, grimacing as she pictured the Hallett Bible, still in Caroline's apartment. "We should never have dug without your permission," she said to the woman. *I really hope she isn't the murderer.*

"Well, now you have, so let's see what's inside that box." Lisa sneered, pushing Caroline aside. She flipped the box back open, gazing at the contents before pulling out the burlap sack. Lisa unlaced the top and carefully spilled it out into her hand. Silver coins, sparkling dully in the beam of the flashlight, filled her hand.

"It really is a treasure," Penny breathed in excitement.

"I can't believe it's real," Caroline gasped.

"I can," Lisa declared, pushing the coins back into the bag. "And it's mine. This is my property now, so the treasure is mine!" she declared, a smile growing on her pretty face. "Come on, let's get out of this gross hole," she instructed, moving back towards the stairs.

Caroline crossed in front of her, striding up the stairs. "Careful," she called out as she reached the top. "The rain is making everything slippery," she explained, turning back to face them. "Here, hand me the coins and use both hands to hold on," she instructed Lisa.

Lisa handed up the treasure and started to climb the stairs herself.

A bolt of lightning lit up the sky, flashing across Caroline's face as it transformed from concern to pure, unadulterated hate. "Ha! You really are as dumb as they say!" she shouted into the cellar, one hand clutching the bag of treasure. She used the other to slam the cellar doors closed.

"No!" Penny cried out in desperation. She rushed across the cellar, only to hear the bolt on the cellar doors slide home. Lisa, still standing on the steps, slumped against the wall, now in total darkness.

"I deserve this treasure more than anyone else in this town," Caroline said from the other side of the bulkhead. Penny could hear the derision in her voice, even through the heavy metal door.

"Caroline, what are you thinking? Don't do this!" Penny pleaded, blindly climbing the steps to press her hand against the door. She could hear Lisa next to her, breathing heavily.

"It's mine now!" Caroline declared. "And I'm finally going to have everything those stupid founding families have always had. Including you, Lisa," she sneered through the door. "Growing up in this stupid town, watching you have it all while my parents worked his hands to the bone to feed us? I'm glad you'll die down there!"

"Caroline, don't do this!" Penny screamed. There was no response, except for the sound of Caroline's car starting and fading into the distance.

✳ ✳ ✳

Chapter 13

"Did she leave us here?" Lisa finally spoke up into the pitch darkness. Caroline had taken Penny's flashlight with her.

"I think she did," Penny realized dejectedly, sinking down to sit on the steep steps. *Well, that explains why she was so eager to come look for the treasure ourselves, rather than getting the police involved.*

"But she said we would split the treasure!" Lisa cried out angrily. "She said that if I made it so we could keep the land, she'd tell me where the treasure was and we'd split it," she declared.

"If you killed your mother, you mean," Penny interjected. "I'm already all tied up this sorry little scheme, you might as well tell me what really happened," she pointed out.

Lisa started to speak, her voice angry, but cut herself off. "I suppose. We're probably going to die down here anyway. At first I tried to convince my mother not to sell, but she wouldn't listen. She needed the money because she wanted to expand the house," Lisa told her. "So when I couldn't make her change her mind, Caroline and I decided the next best thing was to make it so I owned all the land, including the landing site. So I killed her. Caroline gave me the cyanide."

"You really killed your own mother? Just like that?" Penny asked in shock, recoiling. "I mean, I knew you did, but still," she sputtered as her voice trailed away.

"I needed to make sure I owned the land. Caroline said she had finally found proof, a letter from Black Sam Bellamy, that the treasure was buried on the beach," Lisa declared into the darkness. "We needed time to dig, but if my mom was going to sell the land we didn't have enough. So I stopped the sale," Lisa claimed, almost proudly. "How dare she try to sell that land, anyway?" she continued, her voice growing angrier. "That land has been in our family for generations! Who gave her the right to sell it off?"

Penny recoiled at the sudden, violent anger in Lisa's voice. *Wait a second,* she realized. *I'm stuck down here with a murderer. And I'm grilling her about the murder she committed. What's to stop her from killing me too?*

"It sounds to me like Caroline was behind it all," Penny said carefully, trying to get Lisa to calm down. "She found the letter, she gave you the poison, and now she's trapped us down here. We need to get out, so we can report her to the police. Maybe we can break the lock on the door. It has to be pretty old."

"Nope. It's brand new. Kids from town were coming out here and partying in the root cellar. We put a new bolt on it just this spring," Lisa explained.

"Caroline wouldn't have had the key, obviously, but I'm guessing she bolted it shut just the same."

"I'm going to try anyway," Penny declared, carefully climbing the steep staircase. "Maybe I can wiggle the bolt loose." Putting her hands on the cellar doors, she tried to gently jiggle the door, hoping to get the bolt to slide free. Nothing happened. Frustrated, she hit the doors with all her might—still nothing.

"Maybe we can't get out that way," Penny admitted breathlessly, returning to the bottom of the staircase. "Do you think there's another way out?"

"There isn't," Lisa told her, sinking down to sit on the steep steps. Penny could just make out her silhouette in the moonlight spilling through the crack around the door over their heads.

Penny sat down next to Lisa. "Why did you poison my pie, specifically?" she asked, unable to resist.

"My mother was about to eat it," Lisa stated flatly, as if it was the most obvious thing in the world.

"So you were just planning on letting me go to prison for murdering your mom?" Penny asked indignantly. "What, let the new girl in town be your little scapegoat?" she asked, forgetting her plan from a moment ago to keep Lisa calm.

"Of course the police weren't going to send you to prison," Lisa scoffed. "You only met my mother that morning. After she tried to bully you out of the competition, I told her she should go over and apologize, and take a piece of your pie as a peace offering. I slipped the poison into the pie, specifically, so that the police wouldn't be able to find a motive."

"That is...a shockingly well thought out murder," Penny told her, trying hard not to sound admiring. "You fixed it so that the poison seemed like it came from the only person in town without a motive."

"Well, it's not like I wanted anyone to go to jail for it," Lisa explained. They were sitting so close together, Penny could feel Lisa's shoulders shrug in the darkness. "If only the treasure had been on the beach, where it was supposed to be, Caroline and I would have found it and that would be that," she added regretfully.

"If it had really been on the beach this whole time, don't you think that one of the dozens of people who'd looked for it over the years would have found it?" Penny pointed out. Lisa didn't respond.

"Well, regardless, none of it will matter if we can't get out of here," Penny said dejectedly. "I doubt Caroline is going to tell anyone she trapped us down here. Did you happen to bring a cell phone? I left mine in my purse, which is in Caroline's car."

"I left it at the house," Lisa told her.

"So we can't call for help," Penny sighed.

"Don't worry. People will notice I'm missing. They'll look for me." Lisa replied confidently.

"But will they check all the way out here? What would make them think to check the root cellar of Sam Hallett's house?" Penny asked. "Why *did* you come out here in the first place?"

"I happened to glance out the window and saw a car coming down the driveway. When it turned towards the old house, I recognized it as Caroline's and I came out to see what was going on," Lisa explained. "I thought maybe she wanted to talk about...everything."

"You didn't happen to tell anyone where you were going, did you?" Penny asked hopefully.

"Nope." Her one word response said it all.

"Well, we have to do something. I'm not going to sit here in this cellar and wait to die," she declared. "Wasn't Black Sam Bellamy supposed to be clever? Maybe there's a way from the root cellar directly into the house. If only there was some light."

"Here, use my flashlight," Lisa offered, pressing something into Penny's hand.

"You had a flashlight this whole time?" Penny asked with a dry laugh, switching it on.

"Well, I certainly wasn't going to walk all the way out here in the dark," Lisa snapped, her tone insulted.

"Of course not," Penny agreed sarcastically. *Maybe Lisa really isn't the sharpest tool in the shed.*

Penny moved around the room, carefully examining every wall. Lisa's flashlight was much more powerful than the one Caroline had taken with her. She found nothing new; all that was there was the piece of wood she'd used to dig and a row of old, wrought-iron hooks affixed to the wall.

"There's nothing down here," Lisa whined, still sitting on the stairs. "We'll never get out."

"Maybe we can do something with these hooks?" Penny mused, examining them more closely. They were older than she'd thought, maybe even original.

"Help me try to pull one of them down off the wall," Penny instructed. "Maybe we can use it to break through the door, or get it through the hinge."

Lisa joined her. "Which one?" she asked.

"We'll try all of them," Penny told her firmly. "Start with the one closest to you."

Together, the two women wrapped their hands around the hook, pulling with all their might. Nothing happened, and then suddenly, the hook dropped. Penny had been using almost her entire weight on it; she nearly fell to the ground when the hook gave way.

Looking up, Penny was disappointed to see that the hook was still attached to the wall. *But wait....* Part of the hook had disappeared, almost like it had slid back into the wall.

"We broke it," Lisa whined again, looking at its strange angle.

"No, we didn't," Penny said in awe as a rumbling noise filled the room. A section of the wooden wall next to the hook moved back and to the side, as if on a track set into the ground, revealing an old, wooden ladder set into the empty space behind the wall.

"A secret passage. I knew Black Sam Bellamy was smarter than that!" Penny cried out. "Get the journal," she instructed Lisa, climbing up the ladder.

It ended in a trap door, which Penny was able to push open. Triumphantly, she climbed out of the cellar and into the tiny house. She was in a small room, with wide-planked wood floors and plain plaster walls. A square table, with four rough-hewn wooden chairs around it, was shoved into a corner, lit up by the moonlight shining through the window.

Turning around, Penny reached a hand back down into the hole in the floor to help Lisa. "Come on," she urged her.

Lisa quickly joined her in the small house, carrying the leather-bound journal. Penny slammed shut the trap door they had come through, watching as it settled back into the floor.

"You can barely even tell it's there," she marveled, bending down to touch the seam in the wooden floorboard.

"Who cares!" Lisa crossed the room and exiting through the front door. "We're out!" she cried out into the night air, crisp and cool from the recent rain. Penny hurried after her, taking a deep breath of fresh air as she emerged through the door.

Lisa turned to Penny. "I have to admit, you're the reason we got out of there," she admitted begrudgingly. "If I'd been alone I'd still be stuck down there."

"Come on," Penny said, striding away from the small house. "We have to get to the police station and get them to stop Caroline. She tried to kill us, and stole the treasure," she reminded Lisa. She started walking towards the main house, hoping that Lisa would just follow.

"I can't go to the police station with you," Lisa's voice rang out behind her. "I'm not going anywhere with you." She took a step closer to Penny.

Penny gulped. "Lisa, I'm sure the police will believe that Caroline coerced you. That will have some weight," she told the other woman, trying not to let her nervousness show. *Maybe letting the murderer out of the hole she was trapped in wasn't my smartest idea.*

"You can't go to the police," Lisa exclaimed, her voice rising sharply in the darkness. "I guess I just have to kill you, too," she sighed.

✳ ✳ ✳

Chapter 14

Penny gulped. Lisa was stepping towards her, barely illuminated by the light from the moon. Penny was still holding Lisa's heavy flashlight in her hand. She gripped it more tightly. *What do I do?*

For some reason, as she stood there staring, all she could think of was Paul. *That low-down scoundrel*, she thought to herself, getting angry at him for the first time. All she'd been able to think about after his horrible confession, as she moved into the guest room and prepared to leave the city, was how she'd needed to be the bigger person. *But really, there's no shame in getting angry*, Penny realized. A determined grin spread over her face as Lisa advanced.

Without thinking, Penny swung the flashlight, up and over her head. She brought it down hard on Lisa's shoulder, slamming the heavy metal cylinder into her and forcing her to her knees. Staring down at the other woman, Penny was suddenly overwhelmed by absolute panic. *Now I've made her mad.*

Still holding the flashlight, Penny turned and fled, running as fast as she could through the pastures and fencing back towards the main house. She could hear Lisa behind her, but not far enough. *Would anyone in the house help me? Or would they all believe whatever made up story Lisa tells them?*

Still running, Penny made a split-second decision and turned away from the main house as she reached the driveway.

"You won't get away from me," rang out Lisa's breathless voice.

Penny glanced back over her shoulder. *She's getting closer. I have to do something.* Spinning around, Penny threw the flashlight with all her might. It flew through the air, tumbling end over end, until it slammed firmly into Lisa's midsection. She dropped to her knees, staring up at Penny with wide eyes.

Not stopping to chat, Penny whirled around again, racing down the drive. She met the main road and finally stopped to take a breath. Doubled over, her hands on her knees, she listened closely for any sign of Lisa. *Nothing.*

Deciding not to risk waiting around, Penny straightened up and took off down the road again towards town, this time sticking to a jog. Her adrenaline boost was starting to wear off, and her feet were starting to feel heavier and heavier. *I just have to make it home,* she told herself. *Joe will be there, he can drive me to the police station.*

It was getting harder and harder to keep running, and Penny hadn't even covered half of the distance between the Hallett estate and Seashore Stables. She slowed to a walk, giving in. There was still no sign of Lisa.

A few moments passed as she walked, and Penny was finally able to catch her breath. She was getting closer to home. A flash of light caught the corner of Penny's eye, and she spun around, scared that Lisa might be catching up. It proved to be a pair of headlights, rounding the corner.

"Thanks goodness," Penny sighed in relief. She flung her arms up into the air, hoping to wave down the driver and get a ride to the police station.

The car slowed, eventually coming to a halt right in front of her. Penny was reaching for the door handle, ready to climb into the passenger seat, when the car's window began to roll down.

"Need a ride?" Lisa asked as the window revealed her to be the driver, a maniacal grin on her face.

Penny shrieked; she couldn't help herself. She leapt back, stumbling over her own feet.

"Just leave me alone!" she cried out. "Lisa, please, I won't tell anyone," she begged. "Just let me go home."

Lisa slammed the car into park before stepping out onto the deserted road. "You're going to come with me," she instructed, moving around the low-slung black sedan. She opened the trunk, gesturing for Penny to climb inside.

Penny backed even further away. "No. I'm not going anywhere with you. You are *not* going to kill me," she declared, even angrier than she'd been before.

"You're right," Lisa told her. "I'm going to make Caroline do it. She made me kill my mother, now I'm going to make her kill you. Get in the car!"

Summoning the last bit of strength she had left, Penny stepped towards Lisa. "I'm not getting in that car," she declared again. Lisa's pretty face, glowing red in the lights on the back of the car, was fixed in a creepy smile.

Lowering her shoulder, Penny stepped forward with all her might, slamming her body into Lisa's and shoving the other woman into the trunk. Lisa screamed, and Penny may have too, but she forced Lisa down and slammed the trunk shut, trapping the other woman inside. Penny leaned against the closed trunk, catching her breath while Lisa pounded on the trunk from the inside.

"Now, we're going to the police station," Penny declared triumphantly. "Make yourself comfortable."

Just a few minutes later, Penny arrived at the police station, driving Lisa's car with the woman trapped in the trunk. She parked in and ran inside, knowing she looked like an absolute disaster - caked in mud, dripping with sweat, and she still hadn't quite managed to catch her breath.

Penny burst through the front door of the station, only to find Caroline standing at the front desk, tears streaming down her face. "-swerved, and went right off the cliff!" she was in the middle of saying to the desk clerk.

Penny stopped in her tracks. She wanted to hear what Caroline had to say.

"And both Ms. Bowden and Ms. Hallett were in the car?" the uniformed officer behind the desk asked, looking past Caroline at Penny.

"Yes, it was terrible!" Caroline sobbed, her hands flying to her face. "I pulled over and looked over the cliff—the car was in the ocean, and it was totally destroyed. There's no way they survived," she whimpered, running a hand through her short blonde hair.

"And you're certain it was them?" the desk clerk asked again, still looking past Caroline at the two women. "You were able to recognize them in the darkness?"

"Of course it was them!" Caroline exclaimed. "It was Penny's car, wasn't it? And I'd recognize Lisa in heartbeat," she added, wiping a tear away. "It was the cliff on the road heading west from town, towards both of their farms. Just a few minutes from here!"

"Then how did I get here?" Penny asked loudly, still standing behind Caroline.

Caroline's back stiffened and she turned, slowly, to face Penny.. "What are you doing here?" she snarled, her voice contorting into anger. "How did you get out?"

"Oh, so you're admitting that you trapped Lisa and I?" Penny asked, raising an eyebrow. "What a convenient place for you to do that," she continued sweetly as Officer Calhoun stepped out of an office and into the lobby.

"No, I-I did no such thing!" Caroline stuttered, glancing around her. "I saw your car go over the cliff and I...I thought you were in it."

"Now, ladies, what exactly is going on here?" Officer Calhoun asked, crossing his arms.

"We found Black Sam Bellamy's treasure. And a journal." Penny winced as she realized that in the commotion, she had no idea where the journal had ended up. "Caroline stole the treasure from us and trapped us in the root cellar of the old Hallett house."

"Did she, now," the officer muttered, crossing the room. "You've always caused us a fair amount of trouble in the court, Ms. Collins," he reminded her, grabbing Caroline's arm. "Did you kill sweet old Mrs. Hallett, too?" he asked her. Caroline didn't answer, staring straight ahead.

"Nope. That would actually be Lisa Hallett, who is currently trapped in the trunk of her car, parked outside," Penny told the officer. "It sounds like Caroline convinced her to do it, because she wanted to stop the sale of the waterfront land. Caroline thought the treasure was buried there, and needed time to find it."

The officer wrinkled his brow. "Lisa Hallett is in the trunk of her own car? How did that happen?" He waved a hand to another officer. "Grab a few guys and go check it out," he told the other man.

"So, Ms. Bowden," Officer Calhoun said, turning his attention back to Penny. "You're telling me that these two women conspired to kill Janine Hallett in order to find buried pirate treasure?" he asked skeptically.

"That's exactly what I'm saying," Penny told him triumphantly. "If you check her house, I'm sure you'll find a purse of silver coins," she declared. Pausing a second, she turned to Caroline. "Is my car really in the ocean?"

"Brick on the gas pedal," Caroline muttered, still staring straight ahead, her neat blonde bob now looking choppy and disheveled.

"How did you manage that? Do you know how to hotwire a vehicle?" Officer Calhoun asked, raising an eyebrow.

"I left my purse, with my cell phone and keys, in Caroline's car last night," Penny explained, wincing slightly at the thought of her only mode of transportation now at the bottom of the sea.

As a group of officers left the station and approached Lisa's car, one broke away from the group and grabbed Caroline's arm, preparing to escort her deeper into the station.

"Hold on a second," Penny requested. "Caroline, how on earth did you get a hold of cyanide? I'm pretty sure you can't just buy it at the store."

Caroline didn't respond, instead staring straight ahead.

"Cyanide," Penny repeated, thinking over the facts. "You asked me about rat poison, right, Officer Calhoun? Does that mean it has cyanide in it? Because Caroline here is dating an exterminator," she told the officer.

"Is she now," Officer Calhoun drawled in his thick New England accent "Don't worry, Ms. Bowden," he continued, watching as Lisa was escorted into the police station. She wasn't in any better shape than Penny, with a long streak of mud across her face and a tear in the side of her skirt. "We'll get all the details out of those two," he added, watching as the other officer led them away. "Now tell me," he continued, turning to face Penny, "How exactly did you two escape from the root cellar of the old Hallett house?"

"We found a secret passage!" Penny exclaimed. "There was this hook, and when we pulled on it, part of the wall slid away and there was a ladder into the house," she described, her words spilling over themselves in her excitement.

"You found a secret passage?"

"That's what it was," Penny said firmly. "A ladder built behind a wall, accessible only by pulling on a hook. That's a secret passage in my book."

"How on earth did you discover it?" Officer Calhoun asked, pulling out his notebook. "It might be tough to prove that Caroline purposefully left you to die, if there was another way out."

"We were trying to pull the hook down off of the wall to see if we could use it to smash through the locked cellar door," Penny explained. "There was no way she knew about it. Both the doors to the passage were very well disguised. Once we'd closed them, you couldn't even tell they were there."

"Besides," Penny continued. "She came here to report that she'd seen my car, with me and Lisa in it, go off the cliff. That has to prove that she was trying to kill us!"

"Fair enough," the officer admitted. "And honestly, I believe you about the hidden passage. The pirates in these parts were awfully tricky. There are caves and tunnels all over these cliffs from smuggling operations. I guess old Black Sam Bellamy built it, maybe as another way to escape the house if he ever needed to," Officer Calhoun pondered. "In fact, I wonder if there's not another entrance into the tunnels somewhere near that house that no one has found yet," he added thoughtfully. With that, he headed into the back of the station, where the other officer had escorted Lisa and Caroline.

"Are there really pirate smuggling tunnels around here?" Penny asked the desk clerk in shock.

"I wouldn't know what he's talking about, dear," she replied in a kind, bored voice. "I suppose I won't file Caroline's report after all. Instead, I'll go ahead and submit it as evidence" she told Penny, reaching into a drawer and producing an evidence bag. "Glad to see you're alive, dear," she tacked on, almost as an afterthought. "But I will need you to write a full statement explaining exactly what happened." She slid a pad of paper and pen across the desk to Penny and pointed to an empty office off to the side of the station. "You can take a seat in there."

Penny crossed the police station and stepped into the office, shutting the door behind her. She sat down at the desk, carefully arranging the pen and paper in front of her, and took a deep breath. *Well*, she thought, *I guess I'd better start at the beginning.*

Hours later, Penny was standing on her front porch, watching as the sun rose over the trees lining her farm. After finishing her statement, she'd been driven home by Officer Dawes, with the promise that the police department would be calling if they had any further questions. She was still covered in dirt, wanting nothing more than to take a shower and then sleep for at least a full day, if not longer.

Summoning up the energy to move, Penny stepped off the porch and headed towards the barn in the morning sunlight. *I'd better tell Joe I'm back,* she reasoned with herself.

Stepping into the cool, dark barn, Penny heard a strange noise coming from the tack room. She headed in that direction, pausing outside the door. *Snip, snip,* came the noise again. Penny turned the corner into the tack room only to find Joe, sitting on the floor, cutting apart the stitching on the girth attached to River's saddle.

"What are you doing?" she cried out in alarm.

Joe jumped up, the color draining from his face as the knife he was holding clattered to the ground. "You're back," he said, stating the obvious. "I...uh, thought you'd decided to spend the night at Caroline's."

"It's a long story. Now tell me, what, exactly, you're doing here?" Penny asked him angrily, gesturing to the ruined girth.

Joe's face transformed, twisting into anger. "You never should have come to Bellamy Cove," he raged. "This was supposed to be my place after George Collins died. Caroline even told me I could buy it, until you came along with a better offer. You belong in the city," he cried out angrily, jabbing his finger at Penny.

"So you've been sabotaging my property and sending threatening letters?" she demanded. "All you did was make more work for yourself!" Penny exclaimed.

"Yeah, and once I got you out of the way, I'd have plenty of time to put things right," Joe shouted. "Once you were back where you should be!"

"So your plan was to destroy things *just enough* so that I would run back to the city?" Penny questioned him. "What, were you planning on swooping in and offering to take the farm off my hands?" Penny shouted. "Let me tell you something, Joe, I don't scare that easily. I just spent the night thinking I was going to starve to death, and yet, here I am!" she declared, throwing her hands up in the air. "Get out of here!"

"What?" Joe challenged, looking surprised. "Starve to death?"

Penny ignored him. "Get the *hell* off my property, right now! I am in no mood for this. Get your things, and get off my property. If I ever see your face again, I'm calling the cops," she shouted, crossing her arms. "I'll wait while you pack."

Joe scurried up the stairs to his apartment, not saying a word. He returned a few minutes later, lugging a suitcase. "This isn't over," he told her, his eyes flashing with anger. "This is supposed to be my place. I'll be back."

"Get out, now!" Penny shouted. He left the barn, hurrying out to his truck. "I guess I need to get new keys for those locks," Penny muttered to herself as he left. "And a new farm hand," she added wryly, watching as his truck raced down the driveway. The horses didn't even lift their heads as he flew past.

Finally, Penny went inside, heading directly to the shower to wash away the remnants of her adventure.

✳ ✳ ✳

Chapter 15

_____The next morning, having slept for nearly the whole day, rising only to feed the horses, Penny was back out in the barn, serving them breakfast. Without Joe, she was now responsible for all the barn work herself. "I can handle everything with just the two of you," Penny told River and Zion, who were eagerly hanging their heads over the stall doors, looking for food. "But once we get some more horses around here, I'll need to hire someone new."

Scooping grain into the buckets set on the floor, Penny was interrupted by a car pulling up the drive. Hearing the noise, she quickly finished her task, depositing the buckets in the horses' stalls. River sniffed cautiously, while Zion dove right in, eagerly crunching at the grain. With a smile, Penny hurried out of the barn and into the yard. Two cars were pulling in: one, a brand new Jeep, bright blue, and the other a small sedan.

The Jeep pulled right up to the barn door, forcing Penny to take a step back into the shadowy barn. The sedan parked right next to it. Jessie hopped out of the Jeep, triumphantly waving a set of keys overhead, her brightly colored hair nearly matching the paint job. "Good morning!" she called out. "Sorry about that, the gas pedal is a little more sensitive than I'm used to!" She laughed.

Emma and Lucinda quickly got out of the sedan, joining Jessie next to the cars. "Hi, Penny!" they called out together as Penny re-emerged from the barn.

"Hi, everyone," Penny responded weakly, not sure why they were there. She'd just sent their friend to prison—she had assumed she was out of the baking club.

"We have a few things to tell you," Jessie sang out, leaning against the Jeep's gleaming hood.

"First and foremost, we'd like to formally apologize on behalf of Bellamy Cove for everything that you've been dragged into," Lucinda told Penny, her voice warm. "I'm sorry we invited you to the bake-off at all. Although, I'm not at all sorry you're here!" she corrected herself quickly. "Just that you got dragged into this mess."

"I'm not upset about any of it," Penny reassured her. "It's been quite an adventure, that's for sure!" she added with a small smile, still feeling confused.

"After the town found out what Caroline did to you, and to your car, the rest of Janine's friends got to work. They hassled just about every person in town for a donation," Emma began, smiling excitedly. "And we are very pleased to present you with this 'Welcome to Bellamy Cove, and We're Sorry About the Murder' gift," she exclaimed, laughing. Jessie tossed the keys she was holding to

Penny, who missed the catch and let them flop into the dirt.

She bent over to pick them up. "What?" she asked dumbly, staring at the group of women that had paraded into her yard, and her life.

"The Jeep is for you," Jessie simplified. "The whole town pitched in to buy it. We heard about Caroline running your old one into the ocean."

"No, no, I can't possibly accept this," Penny protested, trying to give the keys back. Jessie held up her hands, refusing to take them.

"Penny, you solved the murder of a town leader, and you proved that Sam Hallett was really Black Sam Bellamy," Lucinda said gently. "This whole town owes you a debt of gratitude. But for now, this is the best we can do," she added with a smile.

Penny let her eyes wander over the bright blue vehicle. It gleamed gently in the sunlight, its bright blue hood so well polished Penny could see her reflection in it. The tan interior was chock-full of buttons and switches.

"It's brand new, and it has all the bells and whistles," Emma explained. "The Grouchy Old Ladies may have felt a little...*bad* about the way you've been treated. They were very generous," she explained. "We just picked it up this morning. John

DeMarco over at the dealership even threw in a year of free maintenance."

"Like, it's mine?" Penny asked slowly. "Completely? I can keep it?"

"Completely," Jessie assured her. "It's totally paid off, free and clear, and all yours."

"Wow. Thank you!" Penny looked at the keys in her hand, trying to hide the tears that had sprung into her eyes.

"No, thank you. You deserve more, but this is the best that we can do," Lucinda chimed in, coming over to rub her arm. "We're also here to tell you that we've signed just about every kid in town up for riding lessons. And some adults, too," she added with a smile.

"You'll be ready to start next Monday, right? Because you have about four lessons that day," Emma revealed, looking through the purse that dangled from her arm. "I have the sign-up sheet here," she offered, handing Penny a piece of paper.

"What? You guys...you signed people up for lessons?" Penny asked in awe. "You didn't have to do that," she sniffled through the grateful tears that were spilling out onto her cheeks. "I was going to put up a flyer!"

Jessie laughed. "Well, you can still put one up and get anyone we missed."

Penny looked down at the schedule Emma had given her. "This...is a lot of lessons," she said slowly. "I don't know if I can do this all by myself. I fired Joe."

"Why?" Emma asked in shock.

"He was the one sabotaging the farm, and sending me threatening letters. I guess George Collins had told him that he could buy it after his death, but then I made Caroline a better offer. I caught him cutting up one of the saddles," Penny explained. "Now I need a new farm hand."

Emma jumped in. "I do know a certain young man who's looking for a new job," she quipped, raising an eyebrow and nodding in Jessie's direction.

"Tyler?" Jessie asked in surprise. "I guess it would be good for him to work for someone that isn't his mother."

"Is Tyler her son?" Penny leaned over and whispered to Lucinda.

"Yes," Lucinda whispered back, smiling. "He works in the bakery now, but really hates it. Jessie told him if he didn't want to go to college, he had to work, so he works the counter there."

"He would probably prefer something where he gets to work outside," Jessie ventured. "And you could get away with paying him pretty cheaply." She laughed. "He doesn't know anything about horses, though."

"That's fine with me, as long as he's willing to learn," Penny jumped in quickly. "I can teach him what he needs to know. Would he want to move into the apartment?" Penny asked hopefully. "I need someone who can live onsite, to be here if anything happens during the night. And I promise to change the lock, so there won't be any chance of Joe coming back!"

"He would *love* that," Jessie stated flatly. "I'll talk to him about it when I get home, and send him over tomorrow so you can meet him."

"Perfect!" Penny exclaimed. "Now I just need to figure out how I'm going to teach all these lessons myself. I might be buying another horse sooner than I thought!" she added with a smile.

"I made sure that we only scheduled two people at the same time, no more than that," Emma interjected. "I know you only have River and Zion right now."

"But still," Penny said thoughtfully, skimming over the lesson schedule. "It's tough to teach two people of different skill levels at the same time."

"Well, then, it seems to me like you'll need some help," Jessie pointed out, her eyes flashing in the sunlight. "Emma seemed to really enjoy herself on that trail ride," she said, a scheming note in her voice. "She hasn't stopped talking about it since."

"Emma, would you want to help me?" Penny offered, catching Jessie's meaning. "As a part-time instructor? I know you'd be great with the kids," she cajoled, sniffing away the tears that were still threatening to spill down her cheek.

"Oh, no, I couldn't," Emma protested. "You saw me ride, I could barely get on the horse," she added, shaking her head.

"I can teach you a little more. You can handle the beginner lessons, and I can do the more advanced," Penny suggested, the idea forming in her head. "And half of a beginner lesson is learning to groom the horse and tack it up anyway, which you certainly know how to do."

"Are you sure?" Emma asked hesitantly. "You'd need to teach me a lot," she pointed out. "And I'd have to figure out something with the kids..."

"Bring them with you," Penny suggested. "You can practice giving lessons on them, and I can pay them a little bit to help out around the farm. I bet they'd love it," she said confidently. "I saw you ride the other day. You'll be a big help," she said to Emma, who smiled hesitantly. "I can only afford to pay you part time, though, right now," Penny cautioned. "In the afternoons, when the after-school lessons would be."

"I don't mind. I'd love to!" Emma replied enthusiastically. "I guess now I have an excuse to buy my own pair of cowboy boots!" she exclaimed, a grin spreading over her round face.

"Perfect," Penny said, smiling. "You ladies have rolled up, and in one fell swoop, solved all my problems," she told them, wiping away the happy tears that had finally spilled onto her cheeks.

"No crying!" Jessie commanded as a wide grin spread across her dainty features. "This is the least we can do, after you solved a murder and proved the truth of a town legend, on top of the fact that you were left for dead in a cellar."

"Shh!" Lucinda hushed her. "Don't remind poor Penny about that awful experience."

"It wasn't that bad," Penny admitted. "Lisa and I weren't down there for very long. I didn't have long enough to be scared. Although, it did cross my mind that I was trapped down there with a murderer once or twice," she added with a half-smile.

"Speaking of Lisa, can we talk about the fact that Caroline teamed up with Lisa Hallett, of all people, to commit murder?" Jessie chimed in, crossing her tanned arms as she changed the subject. "I don't think I've ever even seen them speak to one another! How on earth did you figure it all out?" she asked Penny.

"Apparently, Caroline found some letter from Black Sam Bellamy in the town archives that convinced her that the treasure was buried in a specific spot on the beach," Penny explained. "She told Lisa that if Lisa could figure out a way to prevent the land sale going through, she would tell Lisa where it was and they could search for the treasure together and split what they found," she continued. "Lisa couldn't get Janine to change her mind, so she and Caroline cooked up the plan to kill her."

"But didn't you find the treasure on the Hallett property?" Emma asked, confusion wrinkling her brow.

"We did," Penny agreed, nodding. "But only after Caroline and I found a secret message in the old Hallett family Bible that told us where to search. I guess the letter that Caroline found was written before Black Sam found his treasure, or maybe it was just written as a decoy once he'd reburied it under the house. Anyway, Lisa saw us arrive on the property and came to see what was going on, and then she confessed everything to me after Caroline locked us up."

"I still can't believe it," Lucinda sighed, shaking her head. "Caroline was always such a sweet girl."

"I guess the promise of all that money was just too much for her to resist." Jessie sighed. "I heard you found a book, too?" she asked. "Well, really I heard that you found Black Sam Bellamy's 'Book of Confessions,' but I assumed that was just the rumor mill going wild,"

"It was his captain's log!" Penny exclaimed. "Lisa dropped it at the Hallett Estate, and an officer went back to get it while I was still at the station. It was the captain's log from the Whydah. I guess he managed to save it, along with his coins, when the ship went down," she added. "The cops let me look at it. The entries at the end were tough to read, as they sailed up the coast, knowing that the ship was about to go down."

"I still can't believe the Bellamy legend is true," Lucinda said, shaking her head. "Especially the fact that, apparently, Black Sam Bellamy just worried about saving his treasure, not any of his crew members."

"Well, he was a pirate," Penny pointed out. "I think maybe this town has gotten so caught up in the romance of the Bellamy legend, they forget that he was a bad guy. He stole, he killed, and he let all those men on his ship drown," she continued, finally voicing the thoughts she'd been having since the baking club gathering. "I don't understand why everyone thinks so highly of him. He misled an entire town!"

"Everyone needs a story," Lucinda gently reminded Penny. "And he is the story of Bellamy Cove. There's no denying that."

Emma jumped in, eager to smooth over Penny's outburst. "I'm just glad that everything worked out, and the right people are going to jail instead of you! It makes me sick to think that we've spent so much time with Caroline, and she turned out to be capable of this," she shuddered, making a face.

"Well, I don't think we have to worry about her anymore." Jessie laughed. "I guess the town will need a new lawyer. Penny, do you have any other city friends looking to buy a business in a small town?" she asked jokingly.

"Hey, you never know!" Penny chuckled. "In fact, my ex is a lawyer," she volunteered.

"You never really told us what happened with him," Jessie prodded. "Drifting apart? That's not much of an excuse."

Penny looked around at her new friends. She smiled to herself, still filled with confidence over what she'd managed to accomplish that morning. "Well," she began. "He cheated on me," she told them, finally saying the words out loud. "He cheated on me, with his goddamn secretary," she declared into the sunlight. Instead of the pang of fear, and embarrassment, she'd expected, all she felt was pride, at her own actions and what she'd managed to accomplish without him. *Paul would never believe that I did what I did last night.*

Emma winced. "That's my biggest fear," she muttered.

Penny ignored her. "He cheated on me and so I left. I untied my life from his and finally did something I wanted to do, not something *we* wanted to do," she told the group, standing a little bit taller.

"Good for you!" Jessie congratulated her. "I'm proud of you, Penny," she said, her voice sincere. "I may have only known you a week," she added, chuckling, "but I'm proud of you."

"Thanks," Penny said, blushing a little. She wasn't usually one for showing her emotions. "Anyway, our divorce will be finalized soon and that will be that. In another month or so I'll never have to speak to him, or about him, again."

"But I don't want to talk about him," Penny declared. "I'm just wondering who's going to keep that beautiful barn running at the Hallett place. I hope they don't just sell off all those horses."

"I heard from Mrs. Beacon while we were out canvassing for donations that Mark Hallett, Lisa's brother, is coming back to town," Jessie volunteered. "I guess now he inherits everything. I don't know if he'll keep the breeding program going, though."

"And I heard from Mrs. Ellwin when I was signing her grandkids up for lessons that the historical society is going to open a museum in the old Hallett farmhouse, featuring the secret passage that saved your life!" Emma exclaimed excitedly. "Maybe they'll even mention you," she mused with a smile.

"Well, I'm just glad there'll be someone even newer to town than I am," Penny joked. "Maybe next time there's a murder everyone will accuse him!"

"Next time?" Lucinda asked in feigned disbelief. "There better not be a next time!" she declared firmly. "But if there is, I know who we'll call on to solve it!" she added with a grin.

Penny grinned back, basking in the warm sunlight. She looked around at her new friends, gathered in the yard. In the barn, Zion whinnied, obviously upset at being left out, and River replied. Stilton, the grey barn cat, was lounging in a patch of sunlight, rolling in the grass, and Cheddar was inside the house, firmly planted on his sofa.

"What a perfect day," she whispered to herself.

* * *

Penny's Famous Cherry Pie

Penny's cherry pie recipe is a family secret, originally developed by Penny's grandmother. Passed down to Penny's mother and then to Penny herself, each woman has made the recipe unique in her own way.

Pie Crust

Begin by making the pie crust, as it will need to rest in the refrigerator for at least two hours before use. If you don't want to use it right away, the dough can be frozen instead at this stage and kept for up to three months. To use, defrost in the refrigerator for at least a day and continue with the steps below.

Makes two crusts (enough for a single pie with crust on top and bottom)

Ingredients
- 1 c. butter, cold and cut into cubes
- 2 ½ c. all-purpose flour, sifted and spooned into the measuring cup
- 1 tsp. salt
- ¼ c. very cold vodka
- 1-3 tbsp. ice water

1. Pulse the butter, flour, and salt in a food processor. If you don't have one, you can use a pastry cutter to cut the butter into the

flour and salt. Be sure to work quickly, and not to let the butter get too soft. If needed, you can place the bowl in the refrigerator for 10-15 minutes to let things get cold again. You want the mixture to be crumbly and chunky - the butter should not be fully blended. The chunks of butter will help contribute to a flaky pie crust.

2. Add in the vodka - make sure it's as cold as you can get it. Pulse again to combine. We still don't want the mixture to be well blended - pieces of butter are completely fine. The vodka helps to inhibit gluten development in the crust, which leads to a flakier crust. Don't worry - you won't taste or smell any vodka in the finished product! If you'd prefer, the vodka can be replaced with ice water.

3. Test the hydration of the dough by pinching a piece. If it sticks together, the dough can be turned out onto the counter and cut in half. Shape it into two discs, each about two inches high and four to five inches across. If the dough doesn't stick together, add the ice water one tablespoon at a time, pulsing in between. Test the dough after each addition; turn it out onto the counter as soon as it can be shaped.

4. Put the discs of dough in the refrigerator for at least two hours, or as long as two days, before rolling them out and finishing the pie.

5. When the dough is fully chilled and the filling is ready (see below), remove the discs from the refrigerator and roll out to be twelve inches across. Roll very gently, the dough will be delicate. Transfer to a pie dish and fill as desired before baking.

Cherry Filling

While the pie crust is chilling, you can make the cherry filling. By beginning with fresh cherries, you can adjust the level of sweetness as needed, depending on the tartness of your cherries. Feel free to use more or less sugar than the recipe calls for, based on the flavor of the fruit.

- 4 c. fresh cherries, pitted (You can use frozen as well, if cherries are out of season or tough to find)
- 1 ¼ c. white sugar
- 3 tbsp. cornstarch
- 1 tsp. lemon juice
- 1 tsp. vanilla extract
- 3 tbsp. unsalted butter, cut into 6 pieces
- 1 oz. of bourbon - Penny's secret ingredient! Feel free to leave out if you don't keep bourbon in the house.
- 2 tbsp. coarse brown sugar

1. Add your cherries to a medium saucepan and cook over low heat. They will begin to release their juices. In a separate bowl,

combine your sugar and your cornstarch. After 10-15 minutes, or when the cherries have begun to break down and the mixture is very watery, add the sugar/cornstarch mixture. Stir to combine and continue cooking for a few minutes.

2. You may need to adjust the filling slightly to thin or thicken as each batch of cherries will vary slightly in how much pectin they contain - pectin is the natural thickener that many fruits contain, allowing us to make jams, jellies, and pie fillings from them. If you need to thin the mixture, add water 1 tablespoon at a time. If you need to thicken, add cornstarch 1 teaspoon at a time. Remember that cornstarch needs to cook to work as a thickening agent, so be sure to return it to the heat for a few moments after each addition before deciding if you need more.

3. Once you're satisfied with the thickness of the filling, add the lemon juice and vanilla extract. Stir to combine, and taste the filling. If you'd like to, feel free to add more of either flavoring.

4. Put one of your pie crust into the bottom of a pie tin, and add the filling. Top with the pieces of butter, scattered evenly over the top. Finally, pour the bourbon over the top of the whole pie, distributing it as evenly as you can.

5. Add the top piece of pie crust and scatter the coarse brown sugar over top before baking! The sugar adds a delicious crunch to the top after it melts in the oven. You can add the crust as a single piece, making sure to cut vents into it, or weave a lattice top and lay that over the pie. Bake the pie at 375°F 40-50 minutes.

About the Author

Priscilla Baker works full-time in the restaurant industry and is the author of both the North End Mystery series and the Bellamy Cove Mysteries. Growing up in the suburbs of New York City, she spent her time reading, writing, and riding horses. Now living in Boston, Massachusetts, she spends her free time writing! When her fingers leave the keyboard, she can be found cooking, knitting, and traveling.

www.ingramcontent.com/pod-product-compliance
Lightning Source LLC
Chambersburg PA
CBHW050933120626
46552CB00001B/185